ISBN: 979-8-9851676-0-3

Published in Camarillo, CA

www.nadavenport.com

Fairies of Titania Book II

N. A. Davenport

*Magic is believing in yourself. If you can do that, you can make anything happen.*

*-Johann Wolfgang von Goethe*

# CONTENTS


Chapter 1 1
Chapter 2 11
Chapter 3 21
Chapter 4 35
Chapter 5 49
Chapter 6 57
Chapter 7 71
Chapter 8 87
Chapter 9 103
Chapter 10 111
Chapter 11 121
Chapter 12 135
Chapter 13 147
Chapter 14 157
Chapter 15 171
Chapter 16 181
Chapter 17 193
Chapter 18 203
Chapter 19 217
Chapter 20 233
Chapter 21 247
Chapter 22 261
Chapter 23 273
Chapter 24 283
Chapter 25 293
The Tree of Worlds Chapter 1 305

*Also by N. A. Davenport* 315

# CHAPTER ONE

"The key to controlling your power lies in learning how to use it effectively." The voice of Amy's tutor, a gray-haired fairy named Cypress, droned over her. "You have more than enough magic to perform effective spells. If you want to use your magic to its fullest, you must first learn to harness it, not just feed it into things."

Amy glanced out the tall window of her chamber and onto the sunlit garden below, wishing she could be anywhere other than stuck in fairy school. It was kind of funny, actually. What kid wouldn't love to be in fairyland learning magic from a real fairy? But after months of nonstop studying of everything from history and etiquette to fighting skills and casting spells, she was beginning to think she wasn't up to the task.

It wasn't that Amy didn't want to learn spells or that

she couldn't use her magic at all. She could use magic. She'd learned to bloom flower blossoms held in her palm, heal injuries, sense magic spells around her, and unlock magical barriers. But those abilities were what Cypress called "passive magic," things any fairy could accomplish, no matter how skilled they were.

As princess of Titania, Amy was supposed to perform proper spells, the kind of spells full fairies started learning when they went to magic kindergarten. Being half human and having lived in the human world her whole life, Amy had missed out on a lot of magical schooling. She couldn't even perform a simple spell to change the color of hair or summon a magical creature, let alone more complicated spells like growing fairy wings, something she desperately longed to do.

Out in the garden, a group of adult fairies fluttered gracefully to the ground. Their wings sparkled in rainbows of color.

Amy sighed, imagining how free it must feel to fly.

Next to her, Cypress cleared his voice.

She turned to face him.

"Your Highness, if you will kindly pay attention to this lesson, I'm sure you will enjoy yourself in the garden much sooner."

Amy winced guiltily. "Sorry. I really do want to learn spells. It's just so confusing. I don't know what I keep doing wrong!"

"Princess Amaryllis," he said in a carefully calm voice, steepling his fingers, "I understand that, being half human, using magic does not come naturally to you. But what I am asking for is quite simple. You already know how to feed magic into existing systems. You simply need to sense the nature of the system and change it. Make it into something new."

"But I don't know how!" Amy whined. It was a very un-princess-like sound.

Cypress didn't seem to care. He scanned the room, then grabbed a small potted rosebush from the window ledge. "Here. Look at this little rosebush. The blossoms are red, but with magic, they can be any color you like. What color would you prefer?"

Amy shrugged and folded her arms stubbornly. "I don't know. I like them red."

Cypress closed his eyes and took a deep breath. The old fairy did this whenever he was frustrated. He did it a lot.

"Then you can change them back to red when we're finished. Why don't you try making them white?"

Amy rubbed her hands over her face and stood nervously in front of the rose bush. She felt a fluttering tremble of fear in her gut. Every time she'd tried changing a spell or making a new one, the results had been disastrous and embarrassing. But if she was going to fit in with the fairies—if she was going to deserve the title of princess—she had to perform spells.

She took a deep breath and pushed down the trembling in her stomach. "Okay. Here it goes."

Amy reached out with her magic. This part was easy, as simple as reaching out with her hand. She felt the life thrumming in the rosebush; water flowing into its roots; sap flowing along its stems; nectar seeping into the blossoms; delicate fragrance drifting from the petals; and sunlight nourishing the leaves.

She let her magic trickle into the plant, feeling how it responded.

Instantly, the young rosebuds swelled and blossomed, spreading dozens of bright red petals.

That wasn't right. Amy frowned and shifted her magic, trying to focus on the color of the flowers.

Gnarled roots burst out of the clay pot. The stems and branches grew longer, lined with razor-sharp thorns and sprouting dark-green leaves.

"Try harder, Your Highness. Focus your power," Cypress said, holding the pot at arm's length, away from his face. "Don't just give it magic, give it direction, too."

Amy bit her lip and narrowed her eyes. Her palms were slick with sweat. She focused on the blossoms, imagining them white as pure powdery snow, and pushed a surge of magic into them.

The little rose bush exploded into an enormous mass

of thorns, vines, branches, and hundreds of blossoms, all of them red.

Amy screamed, tripped over her chair, and fell backwards against the wall as the thorny bush smashed into her.

Cypress cried out in pain and alarm, dropping the bush and falling to the floor.

"Sorry! I'm sorry!" Amy cried. She cut her magic off from the rosebush, which was more like a rose tree now filling her massive bedchamber, and it stopped growing. "I didn't mean to. Are you okay?"

She couldn't see Cypress anymore on the other side of the mass of roses and thorns, but she heard him huff in exasperation before he answered, "No need to apologize, Princess Amaryllis." He muttered something else under his breath that sounded like, "Far too much magic for one so young." Then her instructor used his own magic and began compressing the enormous thorny bush into a tight ball.

"What happened in here?"

Amy's face lit up as she turned toward the room's entrance.

Flax was there. Her best friend hovered near the top of the archway to see over the mess she'd made. He chuckled and grinned at her. "Looks like some roses exploded in your bedchamber, Your Highness."

Amy's smile shifted to a wince. Her cheeks burned

with embarrassment. "That's pretty much what happened," she admitted, picking herself up off the floor and pushing aside a mass of prickly branches.

The bleeding cuts on her arms and cheeks stung, and she imagined Cypress had also suffered scratches from the exploding rosebush catastrophe. She quietly fed some of her magic into both of them, healing their wounds, then pushed some of her magic into the spell Cypress was using to contain the thorny plant.

When the bush was compressed into a dense ball of thorns and leaves, her tutor turned to her with a stiff bow. "Thank you, Your Highness," he said, tucking the flowery ball of thorns under his arm. "I think, perhaps, we agree that the tutoring session is over for today?"

Amy bit her lip and looked at the floor in shame. "Yeah. I'll . . . um . . . I'll keep practicing, okay?"

Cypress bowed again, and Amy walked to the archway with him, opening the magic barrier to let him out.

Flax fluttered into her room as soon as Cypress left. "Wow. That was kind of impressive, Your Highness!"

Amy glowered at him. "You don't have to keep calling me that, you know."

He made a formal bow, but he was still grinning. "My apologies, Princess Amaryllis. What am I permitted to call you?"

"Come on, Flax! Just call me Amy. I've never liked being called Amaryllis, even in the human world."

Flax faked a pout, folding his arms. "Fine. But only because you're giving me a royal decree."

Amy was about to bite another argument at him when Flax rushed on.

"That was really powerful magic! How did you get the bush to grow so fast? Even when we made the bridge over Starlight River, the plants didn't shoot out like that."

Amy grimaced with a fresh wave of embarrassment. "You mean you saw that?"

Flax shrugged. "I was in the hallway waiting for your lesson to be over. One minute everything's quiet and boring in here. Then I hear a crash and the whole room filled with thorns and roses!"

Amy sighed and turned back to the window overlooking the garden. Dozens of fairies walked the paths between bright flowers, strolled under the shade of blossoming trees, or fluttered over the sparkling water.

"Amy? What's the matter?"

"I can't do spells, Flax," she said. "Not real ones. All I can do is feed magic into things, like a plant growing or a scratch healing. That bridge we made was your spell, not mine. All I did was give it some of my magic."

In the garden below, a handsome fairy plucked a flower by the pond and offered it to the girl he was with.

The girl touched it with a fingertip and the petals flashed from blue to bright red.

The male fairy grinned at her.

The girl suddenly splashed sparkling water in his face, laughed in merriment, and flew away.

The male stood stunned for a moment, then leaped into the air and flew after her, shouting in mock anger as he chased her through the sky on emerald wings.

"Come on, I think you've been stuck inside too long. Want to go to the garden?" Flax asked, coming up behind her.

Amy turned and smiled at him. "Yeah. Sounds fun."

Normally, a palace fairy could jump through an archway and fly wherever they wanted. If she had wings, Amy could have dropped to the garden in a straight shot. But she was half human and wingless, so she had to walk.

Together, she and Flax made their way down the maze of palace hallways, past room after room of quietly bustling staff. Now and then someone would notice Amy and greet her with a cheerful, "Good morning, Your Highness." It embarrassed her more than the name Amaryllis ever had in the human world. Her cheeks flushed pink every time.

"Why does it bother you so much?" Flax asked as they started down a curved stairway usually used for carrying heavy things from floor to floor.

"Why does what bother me?" Amy blinked. She'd lost track of their conversation.

"The spell thing," Flax said. "You've barely started learning how to use your magic, and you're really powerful. Why are you so upset about it?"

Amy frowned as they rounded a corner and started walking to the next set of stairs. Now that she thought of it, she wasn't sure why it bothered her. All she knew was that she felt embarrassed every time she tried to perform magic spells, or when fairies flew around her, leaving her wingless and on the ground.

"Well, I'll have to go home soon. I don't have time to learn all this fairy stuff. What if I still can't do spells when I go back to my dad?" That was all true, but she wasn't sure if that was the real problem.

Flax followed her through the archway to the palace grounds, which was bustling with beautiful fairy folk. He rubbed his chin thoughtfully. "Would your father be disappointed if you didn't learn spells?"

Amy thought about that and shook her head. "No, I guess not."

Now that they were outside, Flax buzzed his wings and took to the air, flying around her like a huge moth circling a flame. He easily could have flown to the garden and back several times already if he wanted to, but he stayed close, bobbing through the air in lazy circles.

For some reason, it frustrated her to watch him swoop back and forth with his iridescent wings.

That's when she realized what was bothering her so much.

"I don't feel like a fairy princess," she said.

"Huh?" Flax landed and cocked his head, confused.

"I feel like . . . like I'm just Amy. Like I'm pretending to be a fairy princess when I'm really just a normal girl. If I mess up, then someone's going to figure out that I'm just me! I'm just some girl who can use magic, only I'm not good at it."

## CHAPTER TWO

They entered the garden together. Here and there fairies recognized Amy and bowed or curtseyed as she passed, murmuring, "Princess," or "Your Highness."

Flax bobbed in the air in front of Amy, flying backwards so he could aim a mischievous smirk at her. "I have a great idea," he said. "I'm sure it'll make you feel better!"

Amy narrowed her eyes and pursed her lips, not sure if she should trust him when he sounded like that. "What is it?"

He landed and crept close to her side as she walked, whispering in her ear. "I know how to do spells, but I'm not powerful enough to do big ones. You have lots of magic, but you can't do spells yet. Together, we could pull the most amazing pranks. Just think! We could turn the fruit trees in the garden into blue bananas, or spell the water so that anyone who drinks it laughs!"

Amy giggled at the idea, then shook her head. She knew she wouldn't get in trouble for harmless pranks like those. Fairies loved pranks. Even her mother, the queen, pulled some from time to time.

"Thanks, but I don't think that would make me feel better. I really want to make spells, Flax. I just . . . can't. How do you do it?"

They had arrived at the little creek in the garden. Amy sat on the soft grass under one of her favorite blossoming trees. Little white flower petals drifted through the air from the branches, like gentle fragrant snowfall.

Flax folded his arms across his chest and pursed his lips as he paced. "You know, I haven't thought much about it before. It's been so long since I learned how, I can't put it into words. It helps to be relaxed, though. Have you been relaxed when you tried?"

Amy frowned down at her hands, tugged a stalk of grass out of the ground, and rolled it between her fingers. "No. I've always been worried that I'll do it wrong."

Flax chuckled and fluttered back into the air, sending up a cloud of white flower petals. "Well, there you go! Maybe you just need to relax!"

"How? How can I relax when my spells always go wrong?" Amy asked.

"Easy. I'll show you!" Flax landed on the bank and crouched by the water. "This spell doesn't take much skill, but it does take concentration, so it's great for practicing. You can use power when you're upset, but strong emotions make control difficult."

He laid his palm flat against the water, and Amy watched as his playful expression softened. His eyes relaxed, like he was listening to gentle music. He let a slow breath out through his lips and lifted his hand.

An orb of clear water came up with it.

"Oh! Wow," Amy said, watching as he brought the glistening, trembling ball of water up so she could see it.

Flax turned his hand over so the orb was on top, then slowly pushed it into the air. It hovered and wobbled between them, casting glimmers of light everywhere.

"Can you feel the spell?" he asked.

Amy licked her lips and swallowed, glancing around. Throughout the garden, groups of adult fairies were coming close to watch what she and Flax were doing.

"I . . . um . . . hold on." Using her magic, she felt the ball of water and sensed the spell that kept it hovering in a shaky sphere between them. "Yeah, I think I can feel it."

"I'm not holding it tightly. See if you can copy the spell and take it from me."

Amy glanced around at the curious fairies

surrounding them for a moment. Then she took a deep breath and focused.

The spell Flax was using was simple. It felt like a pinprick of magic pulling on the water from the center of the hovering sphere. She tried doing the same thing, and the ball of water suddenly stopped wobbling. It snapped to a smooth orb, like a hard ball of crystal hovering between them.

Around them, the gathered fairies murmured to one another in interest.

Flax raised an eyebrow. "You're giving magic to my spell."

"I know! But I don't know how to do it myself."

"It's okay. Just try to relax. This is supposed to be fun." He gave her a calm half smile that only irritated her further.

She huffed and focused harder, pretending that there wasn't a crowd of other fairies gathering around them, watching her, judging her.

She tried making her own point of magic, stronger than Flax's, to pull the orb of water away.

The ball of water trembled. It shook. It spun. Then it burst like a soap bubble, spraying water on Amy and Flax and all the surrounding fairies, soaking their hair, wings, and fancy colorful gowns. Gasps and shouts of surprise erupted from the crowd.

Amy jumped up in alarm. "Oh no! Sorry! I'm sorry!"

she blurted at the fairies, all of them shocked and dripping wet. "I–I didn't . . . I mean . . ." She didn't know what to say. She was humiliated. She'd just proven to everyone that she couldn't perform a simple spell that any baby fairy could do.

Her throat tightened too much to speak anymore, so she covered her face and ran.

She raced into the palace, through the kitchen, and up the stairs. When she made it to her quarters, she huddled in the corner by her bed and let her tears fall.

She wasn't there long before she heard the hum of fairy wings outside her window.

"Amy?" It was Flax, of course. He hovered closer and peered into her darkened room.

"I'm sorry, Flax. I messed it up, just like I mess up all my spells."

"It's okay! You don't have to worry about it."

Amy wiped the tears from her cheeks, but she didn't feel any better.

"Hey! We got to pull a prank together after all!" Flax laughed. "It was a pretty good one, too!"

Amy stood and walked over to the window with her eyes downcast. "What if the reason I can't do spells is because I'm part human?"

Flax's smile disappeared and he drifted back a few inches.

"What if the others think I shouldn't be a princess at

all because I'm not a real fairy? What if I'm queen someday? Will they be okay with a queen who doesn't have wings and can't do a simple spell? Would you?"

Flax set his jaw. "I would."

Amy sighed and smiled sadly. "Thanks, Flax. It's just . . . sometimes I think maybe I should stay in the human world with my dad."

THAT NIGHT, Amy stood in her moonlit room, letting her lady-in-waiting get her ready for bed. Back home, all she had to do was shower and change into pajamas. Here in Titania, she was a princess, so she had an attendant to help her change out of her dress and into a luxurious silk nightgown, mist her bed with lavender to help her sleep, and prepare her clothes for the next day.

Clover sat behind her, running a silver comb through a few snags in her hair while Amy stared silently at the clear blue light of the glow moss in the wall sconces.

"You seem troubled tonight, Your Highness," Clover said.

Clover wasn't supposed to make personal comments like that, but they'd known each other for a long time, since before Amy knew she was part fairy. They'd met back when Clover was working with the Guardians to fight against evil Queen Orchid.

"I am a little sad," Amy confessed.

"What's wrong?" Clover ran the comb through Amy's hair again, the silver teeth gliding through without resistance, and stepped around to face her.

"I . . . I don't know. Maybe I just miss my dad."

A tap at the archway caught their attention. Amy and Clover looked up to see Queen Lily walking into the room with a smile on her lips. Her long blue gown shimmered like starlight. The royal circlet on her brow sparkled.

Clover lowered her gaze and dropped into a respectful curtsy.

Amy stood with a tentative smile, wringing her hands and taking a step forward.

Queen Lily had told her she wasn't supposed to bow or curtsy like the other fairies did, but Amy always felt a little awkward, not sure what she was supposed to do when she was with her powerful fairy queen mother.

Queen Lily's smile broadened and she closed the distance between them. She wrapped her arms around Amy in a gentle hug. "I haven't been spending as much time with you as I should," she said in her warm, musical voice. "It's taking more time than I expected to distribute the elixir everywhere it needs to go. I must do what I can to make sure no fairies are suffering, but I know something we can do together if you're willing. Something you can help me with."

Amy pulled back and looked up into her mother's beautiful face. "Really?"

Queen Lily's eyes sparkled with excitement. "How would you like to help me reopen the Mirror Pool door?"

Amy's mouth opened wide. "I get to see the Mirror Pool door?"

When Amy's aunt, Orchid, had been queen, she'd done everything she could to destroy the doors between the fairy world and the human world. In the end, there had been only one remaining.

Now that Queen Lily was on the throne, she planned to repair them so fairies could collect rowan berries and make the magical elixir they all needed to restore their magic and survive. The Mirror Pool door was one of the most important in Titania.

Her mother grinned and nodded with a light chuckle. "There are many doors that need to be repaired, but few lead to rowan trees. We need one that can provide us with berries, and who better to help than the girl who saved us all?"

Amy felt her face warm and her cheeks stretch in a wide grin.

Her mother laughed, taking Amy's hands in hers. "Would you like to come, then?"

"Yes, please! I'd love to!"

"Wonderful! Get a good night's sleep, then. I'll send for you first thing in the morning."

Her mother hugged her one more time, then strode back into the hallway, leaving Amy to finish preparing for bed.

"How exciting!" Clover gushed as soon as the queen was out of earshot. "Everyone's been talking about the Mirror Pool door. We've all been eager for her to repair it!"

"You have?"

"Yes! Of course, she's been busy making sure everyone has enough elixir. We all know that. But there will be a huge turnout tomorrow, and you get to be part of it! I'll have to choose an extra special dress for you to wear."

"Y–you will?"

In her excitement, Clover fanned her wings and danced across the room to Amy's wardrobe, shuffling through her royal gowns.

"This is a historic moment! The Mirror Pool door is almost as old as the Titania door. So many fairies are going to be there! I wouldn't want anyone to think I'm slacking in my duties if you show up wearing a plain old dress."

Amy almost laughed at the thought. As if anyone could consider a gown from her wardrobe plain! The simplest one had silver thread infused with genuine moonlight stitched around the neckline.

Her laugh fizzled out before it could escape, replaced with a knot of unease building up in her gut.

This was a historic event? So many fairies would be there? Everyone had been waiting?

What if she did something wrong? What if she messed this up just like everything else?

## CHAPTER THREE

The next morning, Clover dressed Amy in a beautiful velvety gown the color of blueberries. Then she tied up her hair in a fancy braid twined with little white flowers.

The kitchen sent up a silver platter with breakfast for her. While Amy tried to focus on swallowing mouthfuls of warm sweet pudding, her mind kept wandering to the crowds of fairies who would surely be watching her at the Mirror Pool. Would her mother expect her to perform a spell? If Amy didn't perform a spell, would the other fairies know it was because she couldn't?

The birds in the garden tweeted and chirped once or twice, like singers warming up before a performance. Then they erupted into their morning songs.

Cool, sweet air wafted through her window as the dawn light grew brighter.

A light rapping against the archway leading into her bedchamber startled her.

She turned her head to see who it was, and Clover dropped her hands from Amy's hair.

"Amy? Are you ready to go?" Flax called, grinning at her from the archway.

"Flax? What are you doing here?"

He put his hands on his hips, still grinning at her. "I've come to collect you for the trip, Your Highness."

Amy pursed her lips and wrinkled her nose at him.

Behind her, Clover stifled a giggle. "I've put a spell on the flowers, so they should stay in place no matter how windy the flight is. Just try not to get your hair wet."

"Oh . . . thanks." Amy reached up to touch the delicate white blossoms. They reminded her of the disastrous experiment with the rosebush.

Clover could make useful spells, like the one keeping the flowers in her hair, and it was as easy for her as breathing. Why couldn't Amy do that?

"Come on!" Flax called from the hallway. "Everyone's gathering in the courtyard. You're going to love this!"

Amy took a breath and thanked Clover again before joining Flax.

She tried not to worry. Her mother was the one who would repair the fairy door. Amy was just coming along to add her magic to the spell. It would be like what they'd done with the Titania door in the throne room, the first door her mother had repaired as queen.

Amy had already done this once. She had nothing to worry about.

When she joined him in the anteroom, Flax was buzzing around like an excited bumblebee. "I've got amazing news! You'll never guess! This is so great!"

"What are you so happy about?" Amy asked, laughing as Flax flipped in the air.

"I get to come with!" he said. "The queen said it would be good for you to have a companion, and since I helped save Titania too, it was only right I should come along to the Mirror Pool!"

Amy gasped and felt the stress wash out of her. "Really? Flax, that's great! I'll be so much less scared if you're there!"

"Scared?" Flax laughed, spun in the air, and landed in front of her with a crooked smile. "You were brave enough to walk through an enchanted fairy door, sneak into Tuleris in disguise, and stand against Queen Orchid! What could you possibly be afraid of?" He grabbed her hand and started walking down the hallway. His wings buzzed in happy little bursts, and Amy could practically feel him trembling with joy.

Amy looked at her feet as she followed him over the smooth stone floor. Her cheeks warmed. "I guess I'm worried about what everyone will think. What if I mess it up somehow? Like what happened with the roses yesterday. What if I do something that embarrasses my mother? Or what if I do something terrible, like break the door?" Her voice grew higher and more shaky as she spoke, echoing off the stone walls as they descended the stairway to the lower level.

"Hey! It's okay. You told your mother that you're having trouble with spells, right? She won't ask you to do anything you aren't comfortable with. And nobody expects you to repair a door to the human world by yourself. That's seriously advanced magic. Even a super-powerful fairy like me couldn't do it." He grinned at his joke and Amy chuckled. Flax was the best friend anyone could ask for, but he wasn't a particularly powerful fairy.

Then she frowned. "I haven't, though . . ."

"Haven't what?"

"I haven't told her that I'm having trouble with my spells."

Flax arched an eyebrow at her with a confused frown.

"What? I haven't had a chance to talk to her. Not much, anyway."

Flax opened his mouth to speak, but then they stepped through the wide arch leading into the sunlit courtyard, and what they found there thoroughly distracted both of them.

Hundreds of fairies had gathered in the courtyard, dressed in their finest gowns made of silk and linen in sky blue, icy white, sunset red, or the bright green of new grass. Light shimmered off their wings as they walked and fluttered around, making preparations for the day's travels.

Amy recognized a few of her mother's trusted advisors talking together by the sparkling white fountain. At the far end of the courtyard stood a group of fairies wearing royal blue and silver uniforms. Her tutor, Cypress, was among them. Four handsome fairies carried long poles with waving banners bearing the royal symbol—a silver tree with splayed branches. Rows of majestic, winged horses with golden bridles stamped and snorted their impatience as they waited to fly.

The moment Amy and Flax stepped into the sunlight, half of the gathered fairies and even a few winged horses turned to look at them.

"So many fairies," Amy murmured with a gulp.

Flax squeezed her hand encouragingly, and they walked out into the crowd together. Amy tried to smile and look relaxed.

"Like I said, this is a big deal," Flax reminded her. "Nobody wanted to miss out on it. Anyone who could come along jumped at the chance." He saw her face and hurried on. "But your part will be so easy! You don't have to worry about anything."

"Your Highness, if you please!" Cypress' voice caught her attention. Amy looked up and saw her tutor waving her over to where he stood with her mother and some of her advisors.

Her mother turned and smiled as Amy and Flax approached. "Amaryllis, I'm glad to see you're ready. And Flax, too. I have a special surprise for you both."

Flax bounced on his toes and fluttered his wings. "A surprise? What is it?"

Queen Lily waved her hand gracefully through the air and turned toward the castle ramparts above them. A wave of magical energy tingled against Amy's skin, and she knew that her mother had cast some sort of spell.

A moment later, a winged silhouette soared into the sky over the ramparts. The creature beat its wings twice, then tipped its head into a downward spiral as it glided toward them. The light from the sunrise shone gold against its long feathers and sleek, furry flank.

Amy's eyes widened when she recognized the creature. It had the head and wings of a golden eagle and the body of a powerful lioness. It was the same gryphon that carried her home after the battle with Orchid.

"It's Sunblaze!" she cried.

Sunblaze landed in front of them with a squawk, wings rustling and tufted tail thrashing behind her.

"Yes," Queen Lily said, stroking the gryphon's neck feathers. "I thought you and Flax would like to ride her to the Mirror Pool."

Amy looked at Flax curiously. His wings still buzzed excitedly at his back.

"What?" he asked, grinning. "You didn't think I was going to fly the whole way on my own, did you?"

"Well . . . yeah, kinda." She shrugged.

Her mother smiled, and Flax chuckled.

"It's a little far to fly on fairy wings," he said. "I could do it if I had to, but who would want to get all exhausted before the fun starts?"

"Flying creatures like Sunblaze have a much easier time riding the wind than we do," her mother added. "That's why we're also bringing the winged horses for the rest of the court."

"Oh! That makes sense," Amy said, reaching out to pet Sunblaze's golden feathers. She'd been worried that riding the gryphon while everyone else flew would only show how different she was.

One of the courtiers approached them with a low bow to Queen Lily. "We are ready, Your Majesty," he announced.

"Good. Then let us be on our way."

In almost no time, Amy and Flax were mounted on

Sunblaze's warm back. Queen Lily sat astride her majestic, winged horse with two of her trusted guards at her sides. The beasts held their feathered wings half raised and their heads high as they pranced through the courtyard, out to the main road in a regal formation.

Crowds of fairies were waiting for them. They cheered and waved from the air all around. Flower petals drifted from the trees like confetti in every color of the rainbow. The air was sweet with their fragrance.

Although she wasn't in the front of the procession, and wasn't even close to wearing the fanciest gown, Amy noticed that many of the gathered fairies were watching her and pointing her out to their friends. Some of the younger fairies, especially the girls, waved at her and bounced with excitement.

She smiled and waved at a little girl flying on unsteady wings who looked about four years old. The young fairy squealed in delight and zoomed in happy circles around her parents.

Then, from the head of the procession, Viceregent Mallow lifted his banner in signal and they took to the air.

Amy had to cling to Sunblaze's neck as the gryphon sprang up like a cat jumping into a tree. Her enormous golden wings swept through the air, her muscles bunching and relaxing at a steady beat under Amy's thighs. The ground dropped under them. Amy looked down to see the flowering trees, highlighted with sparkling fairy wings, grow smaller and smaller as they rose. The wind rushed through her hair, cool and fresh and exhilarating.

Sitting behind Amy, Flax leaned over to look, too. One arm rested lightly around her waist. He didn't seem at all worried about falling. Of course, if he did fall, he could fly back up with his own wings.

To their right, Cypress rode on his own winged horse. Amy assumed he was there to keep an eye on her. The rest of the court followed them, their bright clothing, shining hair, and royal banners streaming behind them.

A glinting river wound its way past the city of Tuleris and out to the fields and forest beyond. They followed it away from the city and out toward the distant sea.

Amy took a deep breath and gazed down at the beauty and magic of it all.

"Do you enjoy riding, Princess?" Cypress asked, shouting over the noise of the wind.

Amy looked up from admiring a flock of snow-white swans soaring below them. "Yes, I really do! It's kind of scary, but that just makes it more fun!"

The old tutor smiled, maybe remembering a time long past when he had been young and daring. "Then you will be happy to know you can soon choose a winged mount of your own. Then you might ride as often as you like."

"What? One of my own?"

"Indeed. As soon as you can master a taming spell, you can choose any winged beast you like, just as your mother did and her mother before her. Perhaps you would like a gryphon like Sunblaze? Or, since you befriended the white stags so easily, perhaps you would be interested in a peryton? A winged deer would be a unique choice, but they are swift fliers and loyal."

Amy's heart swelled, then seemed to burst and drop into the pit of her stomach.

The idea of taming a winged beast of her own sent a happy, tingling sensation over her whole body, but what if she could never do the taming spell? She couldn't be the princess of Titania if she couldn't do the simplest things expected of her!

She turned away from Cypress, hiding her face as she bit her lip and furrowed her brow.

Behind her, Flax gave her shoulder a friendly squeeze. She looked back, and he flashed her an encouraging smile. "Don't worry, Amy. It'll be all right. You'll see."

She smiled weakly back at him.

When they'd flown so high that clouds drifted below them, their mounts stretched out their wings and caught a swift current of air that carried them forward effortlessly. They rode the wind, heading toward the rising sun for what felt like hours. Below them, gentle hills, colorful forests, and open plains stretched in all directions like a tiny model or a three-dimensional map. Golden sunlight glistened off the river. If Amy tried hard enough, she could even glimpse fairy villages nestled among the clusters of trees.

The sun climbed higher until Amy could look forward, past Sunblaze's feathered head, and clearly see the horizon. A deep-green forest covered the land ahead of them, a darker, richer green than Amy had ever seen in Titania. Beyond the forest, the blue sea glimmered. Sea birds soared in lazy spiraling circles on the wind and the air smelled faintly of salt and seaweed.

"It's an ocean!" Amy called, turning her head to look at Flax.

"It's also the border of Titania," he said. "There are other kingdoms beyond the shore."

"Other kingdoms? Which ones?" She wracked her brain, trying to remember the geography lessons Cypress had been drilling into her.

"In the water is the kingdom of Naranda, where the nereids live."

"What are neer-e-ids?" she asked, carefully pronouncing the new word.

"Sea people. You might call them mer-folk."

"Mermaids? Really?" She bounced with excitement and nearly lost her balance.

Flax grabbed her arm to steady her and rolled his eyes. "There are boy mer-folk, too. Just like there are boy fairies, you know."

"Oh, yeah. That sounds so exciting! Real mer-people!"

"And if you look carefully, you might see an island in the ocean. That's Dragon Island."

"Dragons?" Amy leaned forward and squinted at the horizon. The salty wind blowing in her face made her eyes sting, but she thought she saw a glimpse of a dark island near where the sky met the water.

"We never go there, though," Flax said in a low, serious voice. "Dragons and fairies don't get along well these days."

The queen's winged horse let out a long, melodic neigh and tipped its wings to glide downward. Sunblaze screeched in answer and followed, with the rest of the procession close behind.

Thick, sharp pine scent enveloped them as they plunged into the cool shade of the forest. Sunblaze glided side to side, expertly dodging between the trunks of trees as they zoomed lower and lower toward the ground. The air washing over them grew cold and damp, causing Amy to shiver.

A thick carpet of green moss and bright orange

patches of pine needles flashed under them at blinding speed, one moment almost close enough to touch, the next dropping over a sheer cliff to a rocky gorge, then obscured by thick bushes and vines.

Suddenly, the trees opened up, revealing one of the most beautiful sights Amy had ever seen in her life.

# CHAPTER FOUR

Shafts of morning sunlight streamed through the canopy above, piercing the darkness of the clearing. It illuminated the vibrant green moss, bright red and orange pine needles, and light-blue flowers on hanging vines. Motes of dust floated lazily through the air, shining like fireflies when they drifted into the beams of light.

The winged beasts landed in a flurry of rustling feathers, stamping hooves, neighs, and squawks, kicking up small clumps of moss and soil.

When they settled down, Amy slid off Sunblaze's back and stared around to take it all in.

The air was thick with magic. Amy could feel it swirling around her, flowing through her body and tingling over her skin.

Between the trees and disappearing into the

surrounding forest, a shallow pool spread out as smooth as glass. If the air had been a lot colder, Amy would have assumed that it was made of flawless ice. It was so perfectly tranquil that the world above reflected on its surface, just like a mirror, showing a peaceful forest growing upside down in its depths.

"This is the Mirror Pool," she said, wide-eyed.

Flax dropped to the ground beside her. "Yeah," he said, a note of pride in his voice.

All around them, the adult fairies were tending to their winged beasts, unpacking gear, and making preparations.

A warm hand rested on her shoulder and Amy looked up to see her mother standing over her, radiant with power and beauty, as she gazed toward the still water. "This is one of the most important doors in Titania," she said in a low, smooth voice. She regarded Amy with a smile. "I'm glad you're here with me to help restore it."

Amy felt a twinge of uncertainty as she returned the smile, thinking about all the spells she'd tried to do and how she'd messed them up.

"Um, Mother?"

Queen Lily nodded patiently.

"What if . . . I mean . . . can I ask? What . . ." She trailed off, unable to find the words. She wanted to say that she couldn't do spells like she ought to. She wanted to ask if something was wrong with her. But what if there was? She couldn't disappoint her mother, the fairy queen. She was so beautiful and powerful and perfect.

Maybe she wasn't trying hard enough. Maybe she had to practice more.

"What's the matter, Amaryllis?" Her mother's mouth pulled down as she frowned with concern.

"No one else is here," Amy finally blurted. "What if nobody comes?"

Queen Lily's frown melted into a smile, and she laughed. "No need to worry about that, child. They're on their way. We had to arrive first to make our preparations. Come, I'll tell you some stories of this place. It will be good for you to understand its significance before we restore the door."

For the rest of the day, Amy stayed close to her mother while the fairies of the court set up the silver and blue pavilion, fed the flying horses, unpacked supplies, and prepared food.

Her mother told stories of fairy adventurers who traveled through the door to brave the human world in search of rowan berries or to interfere with the lives of humans. She told about great human kings who came through the door seeking magic to build their power and wealth, or to save their kingdoms from brutal enemies. She told how the last unicorn in the world had gone through the Mirror Pool door to escape a human hunting party, and still lived in Titania to that day. In one of the stories, Queen Titania herself traveled through the door to punish a cruel human prince by transforming him into a hideous beast until he learned to love someone other than himself.

By the end of the day, crowds of fairies filled the forest surrounding the Mirror Pool. Tents of every color imaginable joined the royal blue and silver pavilion of the queen's court. Hundreds of fairies fluttered through the trees, wings flashing in the dappled light.

"The sun will set soon," the queen said. "It's time we rejoin the others for the ceremony." She hesitated, then added, "Are you sure there wasn't something else you wanted to tell me?"

Amy blinked, surprised and feeling a little guilty. She sighed and rubbed the back of her neck. Her eyes wandered to the other fairies fluttering around the pavilion. "There was. But maybe it's not important. I don't want to bother you with silly things."

Her mother chuckled. "Amaryllis, I'm your mother. Shouldn't I get to be bothered with silly things once in a while?"

When Amy didn't look up, her mother placed gentle fingers on her cheek. "I missed out on so much of your life already. When nightmares woke you in the middle of the night, I wasn't there to wake with you. When you were learning to feed yourself, I wasn't there to clean the food from your face. When you were learning to walk, I wasn't there to tend to your scraped knees. I wasn't there to nurse you through sickness, to teach you how to share toys with other children, or to pretend that I understood you when you were learning to talk."

Amy swallowed the lump in her throat.

"I think I deserve to be bothered with a few silly things, don't you?" her mother asked.

Amy chuckled and wiped an eye in case a tear had escaped. Her mother had missed out on a lot. But, she was the queen of the fairies. The reason she'd been gone most of Amy's life was because she'd been fighting against her evil sister to save the entire realm of magic. Feeding babies and kissing scraped knees didn't seem to fit in that picture.

She sniffed once and decided to tell some of the truth. "Okay, but I don't think I should be worried about this, anyway. I already helped you repair the Titania door. Is this the same kind of thing? You don't expect me to do the spell myself, do you?"

"Is that all?" Queen Lily smiled, looking like an angel. "Yes, of course. The spell to repair a fairy door is very difficult. I wouldn't expect you to do it yourself. Don't worry, your job is only to lend some of your magic to it. Even that much isn't necessary, if you'd rather not."

"Oh, that's good. Yeah, I can do that. Phew!" Amy

wiped a hand over her brow, trying to look more relieved than she felt.

Queen Lily chuckled lightly. "Very well, then. Let's go. The others may be waiting for us."

They made their way through the rows of colorful tents. Banners streamed from their peaks, fluttering under the branches of the towering trees. As they walked, the crowd parted respectfully and fairies landed to bow and curtsy before their queen.

Cypress flew down to join them, making a bow as he landed. "Your Majesty, representatives from all the clans have arrived. I believe we are ready to begin."

Queen Lily nodded in acknowledgement. "Then it is time." She turned to Amy. "Are you ready?"

Amy swallowed once and nodded. She tried to sound confident when she answered. "Yeah. Totally."

Her mother took her hand, and they walked toward the water together.

Flickers of magic swirled through the clearing as hundreds of fairies fell in behind them. The dry pine needles gave soft crunching sounds as they landed to walk on the ground like their queen and princess.

It occurred to Amy that if she had wings, they would fly over the water to the fairy door. Since Amy couldn't fly, her mother walked with her. And since the queen was walking, all the hundreds of other fairies behind them were walking too. That meant that all these fairies were landing to walk on their feet because Amy couldn't fly. She felt her cheeks warm with shame and, out of habit, looked around to find Flax.

"Wait, where is Flax?" she asked, glancing around but not seeing her friend in the crowd.

Her mother was quiet for a second, like she was listening for a sound in the trees. "He's following behind us. Can you feel his magic?"

She tried reaching out to sense him, but the whole clearing was thrumming with magical power. She couldn't distinguish any one fairy from another. "I can feel a lot of magic here."

"Hmm. Cypress, would you call Flax forward for us please?"

The old fairy bowed and ducked back into the crowd.

"Magic must seem so strange to you. I forget sometimes that you're new to all this."

Amy laughed a little. "It's okay. I'm learning."

A faraway gaze came to her mother's eyes. "I remember how overwhelming the human world was to me when I started visiting. When your father showed me things like computers and telephones, I didn't know what to make of them. They seemed like magic, but they weren't. I thought I couldn't possibly learn to use all the technology of that world." She leaned down and whispered in her ear. "It frightened me."

"Really?"

Her mother nodded with a smile. "In time, I discovered that I was thinking about it all wrong. Once I started thinking more like a human and less like a fairy, I was able to watch television, use an electric stove, and even drive a car." She rested a hand on Amy's shoulder. "I had to believe in myself and be open to learning new things."

"Amy!" Flax bounded up from behind them. His eyes flashed to the queen and his cheeks flushed pink. He stopped and hastily made a respectful bow. "I mean, you called for me, Your Highness?"

"The princess requests the pleasure of your company," Queen Lily said, inclining her head to him.

"I was just wondering where you were," Amy said. "We're about to do the ceremony, and—"

"I know!" His wings buzzed like he was fighting to stay on the ground. "The door is right around those big trees ahead. I can't wait to see you fix it."

As the water's edge led them around a gentle bend, some of the fairies in the crowd started singing. The gentle song hung in the air around them like a soft cloud, hard to hear at first, but growing louder every moment as more fairies joined in.

Though she couldn't understand the words, the song was so beautiful she never wanted it to stop. It was so heartbreaking that she could barely stand to listen to it.

"What does it mean?" she whispered to Flax.

"It's a remembering song. They're singing about beautiful things in the past, remembering them, and . . . being sad about them? I don't know. I don't have the right words to explain." He glanced up at the queen.

"It's a song of lasts," the queen said quietly. "The song remembers the final moments of many things in our history. Moments that we long for but cannot have because they will never come again. The last time we danced at court in the hall of a human king. The last time our kind helped the flowers to bloom in the garden of Alexandria. The last time we helped a newborn unicorn stand for the first time. The last time a new fairy door was created between our worlds. The last time King Oberon and Queen Titania threw a feast in the great hall of Tuleris. The last time dragons joined us in the skies . . ."

"It sounds sad," Amy murmured.

"It is sad. But it is fitting, because of the final words of the song."

"What does it say?"

"All these things we have loved. All these things have faded. And yet . . ."

"And yet what?"

"That's it. The song ends with those two words. And yet. It makes you think there is more coming, something that will change how you see those losses and make everything better. It sounds hopeful, doesn't it? When the song ends, you stop thinking about things lost and face the present moment with those two words in your mind. You think to yourself, and yet what? Then you realize that there is still hope. Something else is always coming right around the corner. Like this." She waved her hand before them and Amy looked ahead.

In front of them, a narrow strip of land led to a small stone bridge. On the other side of the bridge, white stone rubble and thick green moss covered a small island.

Flax choked out a gasp and went still.

Amy glanced at him.

His eyes were wide and shining, his face pale. His hand clutched at his chest like someone had punched him. "I . . . I knew it was broken," he whispered, "but it hurts to see it like this."

Amy rested a hand on his arm.

He closed his eyes, but he still clutched his chest.

When the singing stopped, the queen turned to address the gathered crowd. She used formal language that Amy didn't understand much, with long, old words and fancy court speech. Amy understood just enough to know she was talking about hope and a new beginning.

Amy watched Flax out of the corner of her eye while her mother spoke. He kept fidgeting and glancing at the broken rubble on the island like it was an injured puppy he wanted to help.

She scooted a little closer to him and whispered under her breath, "Did you ever go through this door?"

He froze for a second. His wings fluttered nervously. Then he gave a short nod. "Yes. With my father . . ."

Then she understood his reaction. When she'd first met Flax, he'd dropped hints that his father was teaching him how to be a berry collector, one of the brave fairies who would go to the human world to collect rowan berries. Since Flax was the only fairy who'd known about the secret door to her grandmother's barn—even his mother didn't know where it was—his father must have taken him through a different door to teach him. It must have been the Mirror Pool door, the one the fairies relied on most to get berries for their magic elixir.

"Are you ready, Amaryllis?"

Amy blinked out of her daydream and looked up at her mother, then at the crowd of fairies watching her, waiting.

"I'm ready," she said, and meant it. If restoring this door would wipe that sad, haunted look out of Flax's eyes, she'd do it in an instant.

Together, Amy and her mother walked over the stone bridge to the island.

The crowd hushed.

They stopped on the stone paving before the broken rubble. Queen Lily stretched out her hands.

Magic crackled through the air, like static electricity before a thunderstorm.

Amy grasped the talisman hanging from her neck, focused her magic through it, and stretched out a hand toward the pile of broken stone.

She could feel her mother's spell. Now that she'd been studying with Cypress, she understood it so much more than the last time, when they'd restored the Titania door together.

Then, it had only felt like a surge of potent magic thrumming through the air. Now, she could sense hundreds of threads of power woven through the spell, like a tapestry crafted by a master artisan. Each delicate tendril of magic twisted and worked its way through the others in an intricate dance, harmonizing with the magical residue radiating from the ruined fairy door.

Amy's mouth fell open in awe and she looked up at her mother, wide-eyed. How could she touch that spell? The slightest change would ruin the whole thing!

Queen Lily smiled and nodded in encouragement.

Amy swallowed, closed her eyes, and tried to forget how her spells always turned into disasters.

She let her magic trickle into the spell, a little bit at first. When nothing horrible happened, she pushed a little more in, then even more, boosting the spell, strengthening it. She felt magic draining out of her. It poured out like water from a broken fire hydrant, but she didn't give up. She knew the spell was draining her mother as well. They were doing this together.

She could hear the stones tumbling against one another, smacking together with deep crunching noises. Heavy thumps shook the ground. Startled birds squawked in the surrounding trees.

A sound like a thunderclap shattered the air and everything went silent. Exhausted, Amy staggered a little and opened her eyes.

It was done. An ornate marble archway stood on the island, smooth and perfect. The space under it was completely dark, like the entrance to a tunnel with no end.

# CHAPTER FIVE

The surrounding crowd erupted into shouts and cheers and applause. Many of the fairies couldn't contain themselves and rushed into the air on glittering wings, singing and laughing for joy.

"You did it!" Flax shouted, rushing forward and wrapping Amy in a tight, joyful embrace.

"You thought I couldn't?" Amy teased, laughing at him and hugging him back.

"Of course I knew you could do it. But you did it! It's wonderful! I can't wait to go through it again!"

"Surely, the honor of being first through the door belongs to one who reopened it," Cypress said, eyeing Flax like a disapproving schoolteacher.

"Well, I didn't mean now. Of course the queen should —I only meant . . ." Flax blushed and shuffled his feet.

"Cypress," Queen Lily said in a mildly scolding voice,

"you know perfectly well that I cannot leave now that my magic is tied to Titania."

"Of course, Your Majesty." Cypress bowed. "However, it occurs to me that the princess should have the honor, since she played a critical role in the door's reopening."

"Me?" Amy asked with a gasp of surprise. "You think I should go through?"

"Why not?" Flax asked, perking up again. "Oh, Amy, the most beautiful grove of rowan trees is on the other side of that door. The ground is like a golden carpet of leaves and the sunlight is like emeralds. You'll love it!"

"Really?" Her heart pounded with excitement as she turned to her mother.

Queen Lily pursed her lips in thought. "I don't see why not. Humans never visit the sacred forest. And it is fitting, so long as you have an escort to guide you."

Cypress was opening his mouth to offer to go with her, but Amy rushed to blurt out, "Could Flax come with me? Please?"

Cypress' mouth snapped shut and his eyes darted to Flax, looking slightly irritated.

Queen Lily raised an inquiring eyebrow at Flax. "You've been through this door before?"

"Many times, Your Majesty." Flax puffed out his chest proudly. "My father was training me to be a berry collector. I know the forest on the other side very well."

Now the queen turned her gaze to Hawthorne, Flax's father, where he stood in the front row of the queen's court.

"With your permission, Hawthorne?" she asked.

Hawthorne smiled and bowed his approval. His eyes twinkled at Flax.

The queen nodded back and smiled. "Very well," she said. "Flax will be your guide on this venture through the repaired Mirror Pool door. Go together. Stay together, and don't linger long. We will all be waiting eagerly for your report."

Amy and Flax exchanged a grin.

Then, before she knew it, Flax grabbed her hand and pulled her toward the fairy door.

"It's wonderful. I'll show you!" he said, bouncing and buzzing his wings as he drew her to the stone archway.

The magic barrier under the arch seemed to hum and crackle with invisible power. The runes carved into the marble glowed with shifting amber, green, and blue light.

Amy stretched out one hand toward the darkness, feeling the powerful magic radiating like heat from a stovetop. Though it was enormously powerful, the spell felt right. Somehow, she could tell that it wasn't dangerous at all. They could walk through as safely as walking through the door to her home.

The gathered crowd of fairies on the bank went

completely quiet as everyone waited with bated breath to watch them go through. Amy could hear birds chirping in the trees. In the camp behind them, the winged horses stamped their hooves, ruffled their feathers, and swished their tails, sensing the anticipation.

"Are you ready?" Flax asked under his breath. His eyes shone with eagerness.

Amy nodded. "Yeah. Let's go."

Together, they stepped into the dark curtain of magic. All light vanished. The sounds of the soft birdsong vanished. A whinny from one of the winged horses abruptly cut off. Then Amy stepped out of a tall crack in the trunk of an ancient rowan tree. Flax stepped out right behind her.

The forest on the other side was just as Flax had described. Sunlight filtered green through the leaves of the trees overhead. On their branches, clusters of yellow rowan berries were ripening. Brown and gold fallen leaves covered the ground. The warm air smelled rich and earthy.

"Wow . . ." She let out a breath. "It's almost like we're still in Titania."

"I know!" Flax agreed. He reached up to examine a cluster of rowan berries. "But you can't find these in Titania. It looks like they aren't ripe yet, though."

"Did you want to collect some while we are here?"

Flax shrugged. "It's always a good idea when we

can. But we aren't here to collect berries. Come with me, I want to show you something!" He jumped into the air, wings whirring, and flew around the trunk of the tree.

Amy scrambled after him. "Hold on! Wait for me!"

"Come on!" Flax laughed, bobbing in the air. "There's an awesome waterfall over here. And a boulder that looks like a dragon's head. And a family of foxes! And—"

He reached the top of the rise, turned to look over the hill, then dropped to the ground like a rock.

At first, Amy thought he was giving her a chance to catch up to him on her slow, clumsy human legs. Then he looked back and she saw his stunned face, his eyes wide with fright.

"What's wrong?" she panted.

Instead of answering, Flax clasped his talisman and closed his eyes. There was a flash of light and a soft pop. Suddenly, in the place where Flax had been, a small creature the size of a dragonfly buzzed in the air.

It flew nearer and Amy nearly shrieked in alarm before Flax's tiny voice reached her ears.

"Amy! I need to hide! Let me ride your shoulder."

She looked closer. The insect-sized creature was Flax! His tiny wings made a buzzing sound like a fat, fuzzy bumblebee, but he still looked like a normal fairy boy—tousled black hair, fancy blue ceremonial tunic and all.

Amy leaned forward, staring at him. "You made yourself small? Why? How?"

The tiny fairy flew close, landed on her shoulder, and tucked himself in the hair next to her ear. "There are men up there, and they have machines! What are they doing in our forest? Humans never come here! I can't let them see me."

Even though he was as small as a mouse, she could tell he sounded enraged. His fluttering wings tickled her neck.

"Maybe I can find out what they're doing," Amy said.

"You want to spy on them?"

"This door is important, right?"

"Yes! It's one of the most important fairy doors we have."

"So, if humans come here, it will be harder for fairies to collect rowan berries anymore. That would be bad for everyone. But maybe they aren't here to stay. Maybe they'll go away soon."

Flax gave a tiny sigh and rested his hand on her ear. "Be careful, Amy. I don't think they should see you either, even though you look human."

"All right. How long can you stay small like that?"

"Don't worry. It doesn't take any magic to stay this size. Just make sure they don't see you and we should be fine."

With a quick nod, Amy crouched low and started

climbing up the rise, trying not to make noise as she stepped through bushes and pushed her way through crunchy piles of last year's fallen leaves.

As she peeked over the top of the hill, a loud noise ripped through the air. A deep rumbling sound that sounded both familiar and completely foreign in this quiet, beautiful forest—a heavy diesel engine roaring to life.

Flax trembled against her cheek. "What's that? Some kind of monster? Or a machine?"

The area beyond the hilltop was strewn with the shattered remains of trees. Piles of dirt and swathes of brown mud covered the ground. Men wearing white hard hats and bright-yellow vests stomped about in sturdy brown boots. A big dump truck sat in the corner of the clearing, its bed filled with rocks and dirt. A bulldozer was crawling toward them over the squishy ground on its caterpillar treads while two men shouted at one another over the noise.

"It's a bulldozer," Amy said.

"But what are they doing? Where did the trees go? What happened to the earth? Are they destroying the forest?"

"They're tearing down the trees. I don't know why . . ."

"Hey! Stop!" one man hollered, waving at the cab of the bulldozer.

The huge yellow machine ground to a halt, still halfway across the clearing.

"Someone's over there!" the man yelled.

"Is that a little girl?" another asked.

"They saw you! Run!" Flax's tiny shout rang in her ear.

Amy turned and bolted back down the hill, skidding on the dry leaves and kicking up her skirt as she ran.

"Hey, you! Little girl! Stop!" the man behind her shouted. She could hear his work boots squish and thump into the soft damp leaves as he chased after her.

"Get back to the fairy door! Quick!" Flax squeaked, squeezing her earlobe.

The big rowan tree was up ahead. The door to Titania was on the far side of the trunk, hidden in a wide crack. She sprang toward it. As she was rounding the curve of the trunk, a rough hand grabbed her arm.

"Stop right there!" the man hollered, turning her to face him. "Where did you come from? You're not supposed to be here!"

## CHAPTER SIX

The man released her arm and towered over her, blocking her way.

"What do you think you're doing here?" he asked, panting and wiping sweat from his brow. "This is a work zone! It's not safe for children to be playing around these parts. We've got a lot of dangerous equipment working in this area. Where are your parents?"

"I–I . . ." Amy stammered, not sure what to say. She felt Flax's tiny form on her shoulder huddle deeper in her red hair. "I didn't know. I'm sorry."

"You didn't know?" The man rolled his eyes and chuckled in disbelief. "Listen, kid. You could get hurt playing around a work zone. If I hadn't seen you, Mike could have run you right over with the bulldozer! You're telling me you hiked all the way out here, in the middle of nowhere, but you didn't know we had a construction project going on?" He shook his head and ran a hand over his eyes. "You know what? It doesn't matter. Come with me. We're going to call your parents."

Amy's heart lurched in her chest. She glanced back at the big rowan tree, but she had no chance to get through the door now. The man wasn't taking his eyes off her. She had no choice but to follow him back up the hill where all the big trucks and machines sat idling and spewing smoke everywhere. Several workers shot her annoyed looks as the man who caught her opened the passenger door to a pickup truck and gestured for her to climb in.

She hesitated.

"I'm not going to drive you anywhere," the man said. "You need to stay in here where it's safe while you wait for your mum or dad to pick you up. You have a mobile, right?"

Amy gulped and twisted her fingers together. Would this guy really call her dad? She was in so much trouble!

But it was even worse than that! Her dad was a well-known musician. If word got out that someone caught Brandon Porter's daughter trespassing in a work zone, it might end up on the news. She wasn't sure what that would mean for her dad, but it couldn't be good.

She climbed into the cab, pushing aside a stack of papers to clear the seat. It smelled like dirt and grease inside. "I–I don't have a phone, and I don't know their phone numbers," she lied, but only about the second part. She didn't have a phone. Phones didn't work in Titania, anyway.

The man stuck his thumbs in his belt and heaved a deep sigh. "If you say so. We'll have to do this the hard way, then. I'll call the police and have them come pick you up."

Amy's heart skipped a beat. She rubbed her sweaty palms on her dress. "You will?"

"I don't have any other choice." He reached into the cab of the truck and pulled a black phone off the dash, tapping and scrolling on the screen as he searched for the phone number of the local police station.

"What are you all building here, anyway?" Amy asked, in part because she thought her mother would want to know, and also hoping to distract him and delay the inevitable.

"A company purchased this land to build a vacation resort. This area here is going to be the parking lot. Down the hill where you came from is where the main office building will be. There's going to be nice little cabins and hiking trails all over."

"A resort? So people are going to come here all the time?"

He had his phone to his ear now and held up a finger to silence her. Someone on the other end must have picked up, because a moment later, he closed the truck door and turned away. "Yeah, this is Derek Jacobs. I'm the foreman up here on Pennine Way, working on the project for Five Star. We've got a bit of a situation here . . ." He stepped away from the truck and his voice grew too quiet to hear any more.

"What am I going to do?" Amy said, pressing her fists over her eyes. "We're going to be in so much trouble!"

"Amy, listen. I think we can get back to the fairy door," Flax buzzed in her ear.

"How? They're all watching me!" She looked out the truck windows. Most of the workers had stopped what they were doing and were resting against their equipment, taking drinks from their water bottles and shooting glances her way as the foreman spoke to the police.

"We can use magic. I know a spell that will turn us invisible. I'll need your help, but if it works, you should be able to sneak us out of here and back to the fairy door before anyone catches us."

"You want me to help power one of your spells?"

"No, it would work better if you could do the spell yourself. I can't keep you invisible very well, especially in daylight. I'm not that powerful."

"Flax, you know I can't do that! Isn't there another spell that'll help us get out of here?"

"Not without showing them you have magic! And we can't let that happen!"

Amy wiped her hands over her face.

"Please, Amy. You have to try! If we wait too long, we might lose our chance!"

Amy shook her head and squeezed her eyes shut. She knew it wouldn't work. But what other choice did they have? "Okay, fine. I'll try. Tell me how to do the spell."

For several minutes, Flax gave her instructions. He explained how she needed to think of the light moving around her. How it bounced off her skin and hair and clothes from all sides like beads of hail. She needed to use her magic to make the light flow around her body instead, like a soft wind, or like water moving around a boulder in a stream.

After a bit of concentration, she could sense the light as he described it. With her magic, she could feel the radiant heat, like a warm shower, cascading gently over her body.

"I understand how the spell is supposed to work," she said, "but I still don't know if I'll be able to do it. You know I totally mess up all the spells I try."

"But, Amy—"

A sharp rapping sound at the window made Amy jump and Flax fall silent against her ear.

The foreman was outside the window, shading his eyes against the sun's glare with his hand. "The police are sending someone to pick you up," he said, his voice muffled through the glass. "It should only be a few minutes. They'll be able to take you home, okay?"

Amy's hands trembled in her lap as she nodded at him.

"You need anything?"

She shook her head no.

He nodded with a rough grunt, then turned and walked away.

"All right. I have to try it," she said.

"Here. This might help. Feel how I do it." Flax touched her cheek with his miniature hand.

Amy closed her eyes and took a deep breath, sensing his magic with hers.

Flax's body started thrumming with a gentle spell. She could feel how calm he was, how confident, how completely relaxed. His magic hummed like a low lullaby, and suddenly, in her mind's eye, she saw how it formed into a small, Flax-shaped shield, thin and delicate as a soap bubble.

"Try to copy it," he said.

Amy breathed deeply, trying to be calm like he was. She pushed her magic out, hoping to shape it around herself as he had. It wobbled, but she couldn't seem to make it into a bubble. Was there some other way she should tell it what to do? She tried thinking the word "bubble" and saying "turn me invisible" in her mind, but that didn't work either.

What if the foreman came back and caught her? The police were coming to take her away. What if they found Flax? They'd probably put him in a tiny cage and never let him go!

"Amy, I think I know how to help you," Flax said. "It might be dangerous, but I might know what the problem is. Do you want me to try?"

"You can? You do? Please! I'm trying so hard but I don't know what I'm doing wrong!"

"All right. I'm only doing this because we're about to get caught. And it won't last long. But if I can just . . ."

His hand touched her cheek again, and she felt a wave of drowsiness fall over her. Her hands, jaws, and shoulders unclenched. The knot in her stomach loosened. The entire world took on a dream-like quality, like nothing that was going on was real.

She wasn't in danger anymore. She was playing a game. This was all a game, and she could make up the rules as she went along.

Amy took a deep breath and let it out in a long sigh of relief. What had she been so worried about? Why had she been holding herself back so much?

Her magic was like a big lump of clay that she could shape in any way she wanted. Of course, she could turn it into a shield to make herself invisible! So that's what she did.

The surrounding sunshine dimmed slightly, and

when she looked down at her arms and legs, all she could see was the weathered, torn seat of the truck underneath her.

Amy chuckled. "Well, that was easy!"

"Good, but stay quiet," Flax said in her ear. "They can still hear you. Now let's get out of here and back through the fairy door."

"Okay, sure!"

"Shh!"

Amy opened the passenger side door and hopped out onto the muddy dirt. Her shoes squelched when she landed.

At the sound, several workers turned to look in her direction.

"Hey, where'd that girl go?" one of them asked.

Amy let out a low giggle at their confusion and started walking down the hill.

"Quiet," Flax said. "Please, Amy! I know you feel calm and happy right now, but you have to keep quiet and go quickly."

"Oh, all right," she whispered, walking again. She could cast a spell to make their voices silent to the humans, but that didn't sound very fun. "Hey, I have a fun idea. Do you want to play a prank on these guys?"

His wings buzzed in her hair, and he took a moment to answer. "I would like that very much, but we can't right now. We only have a little time to get back."

Amy smiled and paused at the crest of the hill. "It wouldn't take very long. I could make a spell so they forget where this place is when they leave." She paused and thought, trying to come up with even better pranks. "I could turn them all into donkeys. I could put a spell on their water, so every time they take a drink their ages change. Or I could put a spell on the land, so whenever a human comes here, they forget who they are."

Flax grabbed her ear and took a deep breath. "You really think you could do those things?" he asked shakily.

"Of course. It would be super easy. I could do all those spells and still have plenty of magic left over."

Flax went still and seemed to think about that for a moment. "Wow . . . but no . . . no, no, no. We can't. You wouldn't . . . I don't think you'd like it if I let you do that."

Amy stopped walking and planted her fists on her hips. "What do you mean, let me?" she asked. "I'm the princess here. I'm the one who helped open the door, and you think you're the one in charge?"

"Amy, you really need to hurry. The spell I used on you won't last long. We need to get through the door before it wears off and your invisibility spell breaks."

Amy laughed lightly. She couldn't stay irritated with Flax. He was just nervous. He shouldn't be, though. She was in complete control of the situation.

"My spell won't break," she said, chuckling still. "I could keep this up forever. It hardly takes any magic at all. Maybe I should enchant this dress to always keep me invisible. That way I won't have to think about it anymore."

"You could . . .? But wait. No, we're running out of—"

"Where did she go?" a man hollered from behind them. "Didn't anyone see her get out of the truck?"

"I thought I heard her voice coming from over there," someone else said.

Amy turned to look. The foreman was talking with another one of the workers, who pointed a dusty gloved finger in her direction. "Maybe she was heading back down the hill."

"Come on!" Flax cried. "Run!"

"Oh, all right," Amy grumbled, rolling her eyes. "I don't know what the big deal is. It's not like they can see us."

She trotted down the hill with the sounds of heavy boots stomping after them. She sort of hoped they caught up to her. Then she'd have a good excuse to put a spell on them, no matter what Flax said.

"We can't start work again until we know this area is clear!" the foreman rumbled. "I swear! How hard is it to keep a little girl from running off for five minutes?"

"Nobody saw her leave," someone else said. "I would have stopped her if I'd seen her."

"Are you sure we can't do just one prank on them?" Amy asked, pausing. The big rowan tree was just ahead of them.

"No, really," Flax said, his tiny voice sounding strained. "My spell won't last much longer. We need to get through the door before—"

The world suddenly closed in around her. Everything snapped into sharp focus. The sounds of the men crunching down the hillside after them grew louder. The sound was ominous, like hungry, wild animals chasing after them.

"Oh, no . . ." Flax's tiny wings fluttered against her neck. "Amy? Are you . . . how do you feel?"

What had she been thinking?

Those men were chasing her! The police were on their way! She didn't know how she'd managed to make herself invisible, but she knew it couldn't last! Her heart kicked into high gear and her breathing became shallow and fast. She clenched her shaking hands at her chest. "Flax? Am I still invisible?"

Before he could answer, Amy looked down at her body, just in time to see it flash back into view.

"There she is!" someone shouted.

"Run!" Flax squeaked in her ear.

Amy was already dashing for the tree. She couldn't let the workers catch them again. If they did, they'd probably lock her up. There was no way they'd give her a second chance to escape.

She dodged behind a thick bush for cover, then scrambled on hands and knees to the far side of a tree just as the foreman stomped past. He paused, looking around, then continued farther into the woods.

As soon as he was out of sight, Amy crawled out from the bush and around the big rowan tree. The crack in the tree trunk was waiting for her. She scrambled inside and through the shimmering fairy door.

Panting and crawling on all fours, hands dirty and dress muddy, she came through to the other side. Her knee got caught in her dress and she tripped, falling on her face in the dirt, shaking and sobbing. When had she started crying?

A wave of alarmed murmurs washed through the gathered crowd of fairies on the surrounding shoreline.

"Amaryllis!" Her mother rushed forward in alarm, taking her hand and helping her to her feet. "What happened? Are you well? Where is Flax?"

"He's . . . he's here." Amy tried to get her breathing under control. She sniffed and wiped her eyes, choking back sobs.

Flax untangled himself from her hair and flew into the open. In a flash of magic, he was back to his normal size. "The door is compromised, Your Majesty. There are humans on the other side. It's horrible!

They're tearing down the trees and ripping up the earth."

A shocked gasp erupted from the crowd.

"In the sacred forest?" someone said.

"How could they?" someone else muttered.

Amy nodded and swallowed. "They're building something. They said it was some kind of a resort. One of them caught us and we almost didn't escape. They even called the police."

"They caught you?" Hawthorne asked, looking from her to his son.

"I went small as soon as I saw them," Flax said. "Just like you taught me. I don't think anyone noticed me. Amy did great. I hid in her hair and when the men left us alone, she sneaked away."

"You were both very brave," Queen Lily said, giving them a sad smile. "But it seems this door can no longer be of any use to us."

Hawthorne's eyes flashed from Flax to the queen. "Your Majesty, surely the elite teams can still go through. We are experienced at hiding from humans now and then." He looked from the queen back to the door, desperation in his eyes.

"No, Hawthorne. We cannot risk even your skilled teams of gatherers here. If the humans are constructing a resort in that forest, they will have dangerous iron equipment. There will be many humans in the area. And they will surely tear down many of the rowan trees as well."

Hawthorne gulped, eyes wide, but whatever he was thinking, he didn't say it out loud.

Amy heard Flax take in a sharp breath next to her. She reached out and took his hand.

"Don't despair," her mother announced, loud enough for all the gathered fairies to hear. "I will meet with my advisors, the elders, and learned fairies. We will come up with a solution to this problem."

The gathered crowd of fairies murmured in approval, but they still sounded worried.

Queen Lily took Amy's hand and whispered to herself, "We have to find a solution, somehow."

## CHAPTER SEVEN

Sunblaze stroked her powerful wings through the air in a slow rhythm. Warm wind whipped over Amy's face and blew her hair out behind her like streamers. The soft green expanse of Titania stretched out below them, windows in the tree trunks and along branches glowing with orange light. Rivers and lakes reflected the sky like glinting silver mirrors. Golden and sunset colors washed over everything, making it all look so peaceful and magical that it was hard to believe anything in the world was wrong.

Behind Amy and Flax, the rest of the royal court kept pace on their winged horses. Now and then, Amy glanced back as they rode in silence. Was it her imagination or did the other fairies seem downcast? Had they looked so serious on the way to the Mirror Pool that morning?

Her mother had reassured everyone that she would find a solution to the fairy door problem, but maybe things were more serious than Amy realized.

Amy twisted around in her seat until she could see Flax riding behind her. "Is it really so bad that we can't use that door anymore?" she asked. "What about all the others? We can still get enough rowan berries for everyone, can't we?"

"There are other doors," he said, "but most don't lead to rowan trees anymore. Humans have even broken some from the other side."

"What do you mean?"

"Well, imagine if those workers cut down the rowan tree the Mirror Pool door leads to. Where would you come out on the other side? It wouldn't have anywhere to go to at all. The archway on this side would become just a bunch of marble, leading nowhere. That kind of thing happens sometimes, and we've lost doors because of it."

"But there are other doors leading to rowan trees, right? We can fix them and still collect berries."

"There are a few, yes. But they don't come out close to rowan trees anymore. The fairies who go through them have to travel far through dangerous human places to find berries."

Amy frowned down at the thick golden feathers on Sunblaze's neck.

"But we still have our secret door," Flax said. "The one that leads to your grandmother's house. The rowan tree by her barn grows lots of berries in season. Hardly any humans go there."

Amy smiled and nodded at him. Of course they still had the secret door. The fairies would be okay.

It was too bad that the Mirror Pool door wasn't usable anymore, and that must be why everyone was quiet and sad. But they wouldn't run out of elixir as long as they had Flax's door that led to her grandmother's barn and the big rowan tree.

That night, while Clover pulled the last of the little white flowers out of Amy's hair, Queen Lily came and stood at the archway to Amy's quarters, framed in blue lamplight from the anteroom and looking like an angel.

Clover saw her and lowered herself into a respectful curtsy. "Your Majesty," she murmured.

"Thank you, Clover," the queen said. "You may go. I wish to speak to my daughter for a moment."

"Yes, Your Majesty!" Clover said. She dropped the flowers into a silver bowl on the table and hurried from the room.

Amy fidgeted and combed her fingers through her hair as her mother strode to a high-backed chair and gracefully sat down.

Was she in trouble? Had Flax told her that Amy wanted to prank the workers at the construction site?

Even if Flax hadn't told on her, her mother was the fairy queen! She had magical ways of finding things out.

She thought of all the things she'd been ready to do, just for a laugh, and felt a little queasy. Turning them into donkeys? Changing their ages? She deserved to get into trouble for wanting to do awful things like that.

"You seem nervous, Amaryllis," the queen said in a soothing voice. "It's quite all right, I'm just here to talk to you."

"Yeah? Okay."

"I know what happened today probably frightened you quite a lot. I wanted to make sure you're all right. Do you want to talk about it?"

Amy twiddled her fingers and bit her lip. "So, you're not mad at me?"

"Why should I be?"

"Well . . . because of what happened on the other side of the door. We got caught and—"

"And I'm so glad you came back safely!" Queen Lily put a warm, gentle hand over Amy's. "If I had known that there were humans on the other side, I never would have sent you and your friend there. I should have sent a scout first. That was my fault, not yours."

"I wanted to prank them," she mumbled, not looking up.

"What?"

"I wanted to prank the humans . . . the workers.

While we were trying to escape. I was afraid of them at first, but then I wanted to do things to them and laugh at them. Flax stopped me, but—"

Her mother pressed her lips together, then threw her head back and burst into joyful, musical laughter. Her long, colorful wings fluttered, sending the fragrance of wildflowers through the room.

Amy blinked at her, stunned.

"I'm glad to hear it!" her mother said, still smiling. "That means you're getting in touch with your fairy nature. Pranks are not always appropriate. I advise you to use discretion. But that is how we often choose to deal with stressful situations."

"Oh!" Amy took a deep breath and unclenched her hands. "So you're not upset about that?"

"Not at all, my child. You wisely returned home instead of giving in to the impulse. Was there anything else disturbing you this evening?"

She thought for a moment. "Well, the other fairies seemed worried about the Mirror Pool door not being used anymore, but Flax says we can still get enough berries from the door at Grandma Kerry's barn."

"That's true," her mother said. "The door to your grandmother's barn has turned out to be more useful than I ever expected." She smiled a little, looking thoughtful. "But we can't rely on only one door for long. It won't last forever."

Amy sat up straighter as an idea dawned on her. "Why not make new doors?"

"What?"

"You made the door to Grandma's barn. You must know the spell to make them. Why not make more doors to rowan trees where humans never go?"

"Ah." Her mother nodded in understanding. "I see. Well, there is one complication with that."

Amy waited, listening.

"When I made that door, I was young and rather foolish. I made a mistake. We're feeling the consequences of that mistake now."

"What did you do?" Amy furrowed her brow in confusion. It never occurred to her that a fairy queen could make mistakes.

"The spell to create a door between the realms requires a piece of wood from the Tree of Worlds. When I made the secret door to escape my monotonous royal fairy life, it didn't occur to me that the last splinter of magic wood we had would be difficult to replace. All I knew was that we had a piece and nobody seemed to be using it at the time." She raised her hands in a gesture of regret.

"But you're the queen now. Can't you just get more magic wood?"

Queen Lily shook her head with a frown. "I'm afraid not. The Tree of Worlds isn't in Titania. It grows in another kingdom off our shores. Fairies aren't welcome there."

"But if it's important, maybe they would make an exception. Or maybe a really brave fairy could sneak in and take a piece before anyone notices they're there?"

Her mother gave her a soft, tolerant smile. "Perhaps. But it would be a dangerous undertaking. I will exhaust every other possibility first. And this isn't something that you need to concern yourself about. I will take care of it." She leaned in and kissed Amy's forehead. "Now, was there anything else you wanted to talk about? If there's anything else bothering you, I'd like to know."

"Um . . ." Amy almost told her mother about her trouble with casting spells and worrying that she'd never be able to do them.

Then she remembered that she had cast a spell. When she and Flax were escaping the human workers, he'd done something that helped her use magic better than she ever had before. So it seemed that despite her worries, she could cast spells after all.

She shrugged and shook her head. "I think that was it. I'm just worried that everyone will run out of elixir again."

"You don't have to worry. I won't let that happen," her mother said, standing and bending over to kiss Amy on the hair once more, smelling of wildflowers and sweet grass. "Remember, tomorrow we will be taking you to visit your father and grandmother. Hawthorne and Marigold have given permission for Flax to join you for your visit, if you'd like that."

Amy felt a smile stretch across her face. "Flax can come too?"

"Of course. He's very excited to experience the human world," she answered, eyes twinkling.

THE NEXT DAY, as Cypress droned on about court manners and etiquette, Amy could barely concentrate on her lessons.

Learning court manners was awful. Cypress expected Amy to pay attention, answer questions, make speeches, stand and walk correctly, and make curtsies like a real fairy princess ought to. She was getting better, but it was hard to remember which words to use, what kind of curtsy to make, who she should address first at royal events, or which dances she should join in on and which she shouldn't. And she was sure she'd never be able to dance as gracefully as the fairies did.

When etiquette was over, they moved on to fairy history. Alliances and enemies, betrayals and truces, locations and dates. It would have been tiresome at any time, but now all she wanted to do was go back to her grandmother's farm with Flax and show him all her favorite things about the human world. She couldn't concentrate on all the different names and dates, let alone remember them.

"In ancient times, the dragons, nereids, changelings, and fairies lived together in relative peace. So long as the dragons didn't singe fairy wings, changelings didn't mimic fairies or nereids without consent, and fairies didn't steal treasure, we all got along." Cypress had his eyes half closed and his hands folded in his lap, like he was visualizing the story in his mind. "But, as time passed, minor infractions built up and tensions rose between our kinds. In the end, the dragons broke faith and attacked Titania, forcing Queen Laurel and King Sage to cast them out . . . are you listening, Your Highness?"

"Huh?" Amy blinked and lifted her chin off her hand. "Um . . . of course. Dragons attacked the king and queen because . . . they stole dragon treasure?"

Cypress slapped his knee in frustration. "Your grandparents never would have stolen dragon treasure! The dragons attacked without provocation. Some fairies may have pranked them, making it appear that their hordes disappeared. But no fairies in their right minds would invoke an onus with a dragon by taking valuables from them."

"Wait, what?"

Cypress steepled his fingers and took a slow breath.

"As I have explained already, an onus is a magically binding contract between—"

"No, the part about my grandparents!" Amy interrupted. "You said the king and queen, then you said my grandparents."

He lifted his eyebrows. "Queen Laurel and King Sage were your mother's parents and ruled Titania in the time of the Dragon Wars. Surely you knew this."

Amy shook her head. "What happened to them?"

A soft sound came from the archway. Amy and Cypress looked up to see the queen standing there, her hands folded at her waist and her colorful wings resting against her back. Two royal guards stood behind her.

"They died trying to make peace," she said, her voice soft, "but perhaps that is a lesson better left for another time."

Cypress bowed. "Your Majesty, the princess seems eager for her excursion today."

Her mother smiled and held out a hand to beckon her. "Are you ready to go, then?"

"Yes!" Amy jumped up and ran across the room, putting her boring fairy school lessons out of her mind. "This is going to be great! I can't wait to show Flax everything. He's never ridden in a car before, has he? What about popcorn? What about cartoons?"

Her mother laughed and her iridescent wings fluttered. "I don't believe he has experienced any of those things. I'm sure he'll be delighted."

It was a much smaller procession that went to the secret fairy door by the river. Rather than crowds of courtiers, minstrels, and royal guards, it was only the queen, her personal bodyguards, a handful of skilled berry collectors, Amy, and Flax.

Until the last battle that had ended with Amy's mother ascending to the throne, only Flax ever went through the secret door. Now, a select few fairies knew where it was. The queen kept it a secret from most fairies because she didn't want hundreds of mischief-makers pulling pranks on Amy's father and grandmother.

Sunblaze carried Amy while Flax flew beside them over fields, forests, and between the snow-frosted peaks of Mount Oberon. On the way there, Amy chatted with Flax, telling him about the many wonderful things she wanted to show him on the human side of the door. He'd been to the human world before, but she was pretty sure he'd only ever visited the rowan trees to collect berries. How fun would it be to see his reaction to human things that didn't exist in Titania? And what fun they would have together! They could cast spells to make the hay grow in silly patterns and tell her grandmother that aliens visited her field. Flax could teach her how to understand what the farm animals were saying to each other. They could write secret messages to each other using ancient fairy runes.

As they flew over Lake Village and followed the river upstream, Amy was bursting with exciting ideas. Her father was probably waiting for them on the other side of the door. He would be so happy to see her, and she couldn't wait to throw herself into his arms and have him swing her around in the air like he always did. Grandma Kerry probably had some of her amazing rhubarb and cinnamon cake ready in the kitchen, hot and soft with crumbly brown sugar topping.

At a bend in the river some way upstream, they touched down in a flurry of wind, leaves, and splashing clear water. Sunblaze shook out her golden wings before folding them against her back and lashing her long, tufted tail.

Amy slid to the gravel bank, grinning and bouncing on her feet with delight.

"Oh, I just remembered! Escalators!" she said, gleefully.

Flax raised a curious eyebrow at her, grinning back.

"We need to visit the mall so you can ride an escalator," she explained. "I bet you'll think that's cool. It's like stairs, but they move by themselves. Elevators do that, too, but I don't like them because they close you in. And if we go to the mall, there's a shop that sells amazing sticky cinnamon rolls. You'll love it!"

"I bet I will! Do humans really have machines that can fly? I want to ride on one. And what about a tool that makes you breathe underwater? I never could get that spell to work right. I want to swim like a fish!"

He took her hand. They were about to spring through the door together when Hawthorne reached out and grabbed Flax's shoulder. "Hold on there, little imp! Aren't you forgetting something?"

Flax blinked once in confusion, then slapped his forehead. "Oh, right. My disguise! Sorry, I just got excited."

Queen Lily laughed and stepped forward, her eyes twinkling, and rested a hand on Flax's head. At first, it didn't look like anything was happening. Then there was a flash of blinding golden light that left Amy blinking spots out of her vision.

When she could see again, Flax still stood in front of her. He looked different, but at first she wasn't sure how. He had the same black hair that fell over his forehead, the same smooth tan skin. His face was as perfect as it always had been. And his ears . . . she blinked and looked again. They were rounded now, like a human's.

Flax turned in a circle, craning his neck to look over his shoulders, and Amy saw that his glistening transparent wings had vanished. He looked like a human now.

"Wow! That had to be powerful magic!" Amy said,

eyeing Flax and then her mother. "How did you do that?"

Queen Lily smiled and winked at her. "I've had a lot of practice with that spell. I used to do it on myself often."

"Do you need any extra elixir?" Hawthorne asked, rummaging in his bag and pulling out a couple of glowing purple vials. "I don't want you two to run out while you're there."

"We have plenty," Flax said, removing his hand from feeling his rounded ear to pat the drawstring pouch on his belt. Tinkling glass sounds came from inside.

After giving hugs and saying goodbye all around, Amy and Flax turned back to the dark hollow under the tree root that led to the secret fairy door. Amy led the way, with Flax following close behind her. Darkness closed in after a couple of steps, and she reached out with her hand to find the wooden door hidden in the shadows. But instead of old rough planks and a wooden handle, her fingers brushed up against stony soil and damp moss.

She patted the dirt with her hands, feeling all around, but all she found was more soft dirt and tree roots.

"What's the matter?" Flax asked behind her.

"I can't find the door!" she said. Her voice sounded hollow in the darkness.

"What do you mean? It should be right there."

"But it's not! I can't feel it."

"Can I try?" Flax reached around her and felt the wall of dirt in front of them. "Maybe some dirt covered it during the spring floods." He scrabbled with both hands and thumped his fists into the dirt, but he found nothing but more wet dirt and flaking tree bark.

The fairy door wasn't there.

## CHAPTER EIGHT

They flew in somber silence over Mount Oberon back to the royal palace.

Everyone, even Queen Lily, had tried and failed to find the fairy door. In the end, they had to admit the truth.

It was gone.

The door that Queen Lily had made herself. The one that let her meet Amy's father. The door that Flax had discovered and gone through to collect rowan berries to help save the fairies of Titania. The door that led to the barn where he'd met Amy. The door that Amy had opened, letting her into Titania for the first time.

As they landed on the wide balcony outside the throne room, Amy's mother broke the silence.

"Zinnia, I need you to go through the Titania door. Use a telephone to call Kerry Porter. We need to find out what has happened." She sighed and added thoughtfully, "Perhaps the door only needs to be repaired from the human side."

"Yes, Your Majesty." Zinnia bowed and marched away.

"Can I go?" Amy asked, tugging on her mother's hand. "I want to know what happened, too."

"No, Amaryllis. It's too dangerous," she said, gently but firmly. "I will let you know what we learn when I can."

Heat crept up Amy's neck and into her cheeks. Her mother thought that she couldn't handle going through a fairy door to listen to a phone call? She'd practically said so right in front of the palace guards. If they hadn't already thought of her as helpless, they would now.

"Cypress!" Her mother waved the old fairy closer. "Please escort Amaryllis to her quarters, then join us in the conference room. I'm calling an emergency meeting of the elders and clan leaders. We could use your counsel."

"Of course, Your Majesty." Cypress bowed and took Amy's elbow, guiding her through the throne room to her chambers.

"But . . . what about . . ." Amy stammered and tried to turn back, cheeks still flaming. She looked for Flax, but her friend must have gone home when she wasn't paying attention. She didn't see him anywhere.

"Hush, now, Your Highness. Your mother has some problems to solve that affect a lot of fairies. You need to give her space to think."

"But what if something happened to my grandmother? Or my father? Will we be able to get enough berries for everyone? How am I supposed to get home?" she protested.

"I'm sure the queen is as concerned about these things as you are. All the more reason to stay out of her way."

They walked through the anteroom and paused outside Amy's chambers. "Just stay here for now. I'll have Chive send up some food for you from the kitchen."

"But—"

"Please don't argue, Princess. I must go to the council room now. You will learn everything you need to know in time."

Amy stepped into her room with a pout.

Cypress turned and left without another word.

Amy growled in frustration and paced to her bed, flopping down on her thick, silky cushions.

She hated not knowing what was happening. What if the fairy door was broken forever? What would become of the fairies if they couldn't get rowan berries? Without the secret door or the Mirror Pool door, would they run out of elixir and die? They were right back where they had been when Queen Orchid was destroying all the fairy doors.

A soft gust of wind and light tapping on stone caught her attention.

She lifted her head to look out her window.

Flax hovered right on the other side. His wings were whirring so fast they were nearly invisible except for the glimmering rainbow of light shimmering through them.

"Hi, Amy. Can I come in?" he asked.

"Yeah." Amy went to the window and touched the stone frame, releasing the barrier spell to let him through. "Where did you go? I thought someone sent you home."

He smiled crookedly and crossed his arms. "No one ever actually told me to go home. They didn't get a chance to. I was already gone. So I'm not breaking any rules by sticking around."

Amy scrunched her eyes at him. "Isn't that kind of—I don't know—bad?"

Flax snorted. "Not for fairies. Trust me, we're all about following rules. If a fairy leaves a way for you to do something, there's nothing wrong with taking advantage of it. In fact, we see it as weakness if you can't think your way out of things when you want to."

"What? Really?"

He shrugged, then laced his fingers behind his head and leaned against the wall with a satisfied smile. "Sure.

Our magic binds us to our agreements, but only to what we actually say we'll do. So the smarter we are at thinking of ways out of trouble, the better. Of course, it's best to not make bargains in the first place. And not to be around when someone is about to tell you to do something you don't want to."

Amy furrowed her brow and tapped her finger against her lips. "So, for example, my mother never actually told me I had to stay in my chambers."

Flax looked up. "She didn't?"

Amy grinned at him. "No, she didn't. She just told Cypress to bring me here."

He pushed away from the wall and gestured around at her richly decorated room. "So, do you want to stay in here?"

"No way!"

His grin broadened. "Do you want to go find out what they're saying?"

"Yeah! But . . . oh, wait." She frowned. "Wouldn't it be eavesdropping to listen in? That's one of those things Cypress says princesses shouldn't do."

Flax nodded thoughtfully. "I see. But eavesdropping isn't always bad, is it? If I hadn't been listening in on my father's meetings with the Guardians, I never would have joined them. I wouldn't have trained as a berry gatherer. You never would have met me. And we never would have saved Titania. But I listened because I wanted to help, not because I wanted to betray them." He turned and looked her in the eyes with his jaw set. "You don't want to betray them, do you?"

"Of course not."

"Do you want to help?"

"Yes!"

He planted his hands on his hips and shrugged. "Then what are we going to do?"

Amy glanced out the archway that led to the anteroom and bit her lip. She thought for a moment, then she nodded. "Okay. Let's find out what's going on. Follow me."

The two of them slipped through the hallways as quiet as mice, but it didn't seem like they needed to hide at all. When the palace staff saw them, nobody said anything or tried to stop them. When they made it to the long corridor that led to the council room, Amy recognized two of the queen's guards stationed on either side of the aisle.

"Hello Zinnia. Hi Pine." She flashed them her brightest smile.

"Good afternoon, Princess," Zinnia answered, and Pine inclined his head in a small bow.

"Could Flax and I get through? We'd like to visit the library."

"My apologies, Your Highness. The queen has given

strict instructions that no one is permitted to enter this hallway until her conference has ended."

"Oh. Okay." Amy tried not to look too disappointed as she and Flax walked past and turned down the next aisle.

"What now?" Flax asked. "Pine and Zinnia will never let us through."

"I know. I was hoping they'd let us go to the library. If I had wings, then maybe we could hover outside the window . . . wait. You have wings. Could you carry me across?"

Flax sighed. "I could spell my wings to be quiet and hover outside the window. But I wouldn't be able to carry you out there for long." He grimaced. "I'm not that strong."

Amy looked at him. "So you think you could carry me over there?"

"I'm sure I could, but, like I said, not for very long. Not long enough to hear much."

Amy ran to the nearest balcony, and Flax followed her. From there, they had a view of the outside wall of the council room. Through the windows, she could see her mother's red hair and flashes of fairy wings as the members of the council talked. They were too far away to hear anything, though.

Amy pointed to the empty window to the right of the

council room. "Can you carry me through that window?"

Flax fluttered his wings and eyed the distant window thoughtfully. "It's a little far. But I suppose I could."

"All right, let's try it!"

At Amy's encouragement, Flax grabbed her under her arms and fanned his wings with all his might. Amy could feel him straining, as his wing muscles had to work twice as hard as they normally did. With a powerful whoosh of wind, Flax jumped into the air, his arms gripping tight around her ribcage.

The flight to the far window took only took a few seconds. They landed, stumbling to the hard stone floor in a dim room lined with bookshelves and chairs.

"There!" Flax panted, shaking out his arms. "See? I knew I could do it." He gasped for a few more breaths. "But I don't think we can listen in from this room."

"I think we can," Amy said, rubbing her sore rib cage where he'd squeezed her.

Then she held a finger to her lips in a sign to stay quiet. "Follow me," she whispered.

She led him over to a corner of the room, near the bottom shelf of a collection of ancient musty books. There, she kneeled down and pulled one of the heavy tomes off the shelf, revealing a crack in the stone wall.

"Cypress brings me here to study runes and geography," she whispered. "I got bored once and started pulling books out to look through them. That's when I found this. You can sometimes hear the cleaning fairies working in the conference room through this crack. I bet we can hear them talking if we listen."

Flax pressed his lips together and nodded, impressed.

Amy pointed at the small gap in the stone, and they bent their heads together to listen.

The first voice they heard was Hawthorne's. "Whoever goes through to make repairs must know how to blend in with the human world. Even though Cypress is more skilled with runes than any fairy in Titania—except for you, Your Majesty—he has never learned how to navigate the human world."

Flax sniggered quietly. "Cypress trying to hide in the human world would be like a donkey trying to hide in a flowerbed."

"Shh! I want to listen!" Amy hissed.

Another voice spoke. "Perhaps Zinnia could escort him. She is excellent at human disguise and knows how to use many of their tools."

"It would take more than disguise," the queen said. "It would take navigating their roadways, using their money, flying across the ocean on an airplane, and forging convincing documents." She sighed. "If only I could go myself. But we still don't know what's wrong with the door. Perhaps it's nothing serious.

Maybe the wood has only shifted. In that case, the runes would not need repair at all and we can send the fairy who is most comfortable in the human world."

"I wonder if that could be it," Flax murmured in Amy's ear. "Could a little change like that make the door disappear?"

Amy was about to say something when another voice came through the crack.

"I'm afraid that isn't the case, Your Majesty."

"Zinnia, you've returned!" the queen said, sounding a little relieved. "What can you tell us?"

"I used a telephone machine to speak with Kerry Porter, as you instructed. She is quite distressed. It seems a worker came to cut hay in her field and his machine collided with the corner of the barn. I'm afraid it has broken the door beyond repair."

The silence that followed her speech stretched on for a long time.

Amy held her breath, waiting to hear what her mother would say.

"But . . . surely it can't have been destroyed!" Cypress said.

"We must at least try to fix it!" another voice cried out.

"Maybe we can use the Mirror Pool door at night, when humans won't be there," someone else said.

"There are still berries through the Smoketree Door, aren't there?" someone else asked.

"No, they've built houses all over that forest. It's much too dangerous now," someone else answered.

Amy looked at Flax. His wide eyes matched hers in alarm. "It isn't just about the secret door," she whispered. "They're worried about getting rowan berries."

"Enough!" Queen Lily said, her voice loud and commanding.

Everyone fell silent.

"I know this comes as a shock to us all, but we must keep our heads. There is a way to solve this problem, but it is perilous. I was hoping it wouldn't come to this, and I'm afraid I can't do it alone."

"We are all here for you, Your Majesty," someone said in a subdued voice.

There was another long stretch of silence.

"We must create new doors to the human world," Queen Lily said. "In order to do that, someone must collect wood from the Tree of Worlds."

Amy could almost feel the tension in the room rise at her mother's words. Everyone's voices kicked up in volume and they all started talking at once.

"The Tree of Worlds! But we can't go there!"

"Impossible!"

"It's a death sentence!"

"Who would be foolish enough to even try?"

"I understand," Queen Lily said. "I will not risk any of your lives on something I'm not willing to do myself. And since I am the most powerful fairy in Titania, I must be the one to go. I will need help to—"

"No! Your Majesty, you mustn't!" someone cried.

"It's far too dangerous!" Hawthorne agreed.

"We need you here," someone else said.

"Please, Your Majesty," Cypress said. "If you are caught on their land without good cause, it will be seen as an act of war. You will put all of Titania at risk if you do this."

"They would not catch me," the queen answered in a hard voice.

"No one doubts your power or courage, Your Majesty," Hawthorne said. "But how can you be certain they wouldn't discover you? If they did, think what would happen. Your small daughter would ascend to the throne and immediately face war with the fiercest foe imaginable. Is it worth that risk?"

There was silence, and then Amy heard her mother sigh. "No. It is not worth that risk. So we must send a small team of brave, powerful fairies to sneak in and collect the material we need."

The others said nothing.

"Fairies who will not, if captured, give cause for war if it is discovered who they are," the queen said. "Is anyone here willing?"

There was a moment of quiet, thoughtful murmuring from the other fairies.

"Further," she continued, "the throne will owe a debt of gratitude to the heroes who embark on this quest, a debt that can never be repaid."

Flax gasped in shock.

"What is it?" Amy asked.

"Did you hear what she just said?"

"It sounded like she said she wouldn't repay the heroes for saving us. But that doesn't seem right."

"No," Flax whispered. "It means she can't repay the debt. Once a debt is repaid, she wouldn't owe it anymore. But if she can't repay it, she'll always owe it. So whoever volunteers could ask for favors from Queen Lily forever."

"You mean my mother would have to do whatever they said?"

"Kind of. Anything within her power, as long as she isn't breaking any other oaths she's taken."

They continued listening at the crack in the wall for a while longer, waiting to see who would volunteer to go on the dangerous mission and become a national hero. But while many of the fairies suggested others as the best choice, nobody seemed willing to volunteer themselves.

After a while, Amy asked Flax to fly her back to the

balcony across the way so they could go back to her chambers.

A silver platter of food was waiting on her table when they arrived. Flax removed the domed cover and started helping himself to the bowl of cut fruit and warm, buttery bread underneath.

"I'm sure someone will volunteer," he said around a mouthful of food. "I mean, I would go if I were them! Sure it would be dangerous. But it's important. Without new doors to get rowan berries, how will we live?"

"Without a new fairy door to my grandma's house, how will I ever get home to my dad again?"

Flax blinked at her. "Oh, yeah. There's that too. But I wouldn't mind if you stayed here forever. Anyway, I think you could make it back through the Titania door if you had to."

Amy grabbed a handful of purple berries and popped a couple of them in her mouth. Whatever they were, they tasted sweet and full of delicious juice. "Maybe we should do it."

"Hmm?" Flax looked up in the middle of taking a bite of bread.

"You and me. We could go to the Tree of Worlds and get some wood. It sounds simple enough. We helped defeat Queen Orchid together. This couldn't be harder than that."

His eyes widened for a moment, then flashed to the anteroom behind her.

"That is out of the question!" Cypress snapped.

Amy jumped and whirled around to see her tutor fanning his wings in agitation. "It's a dangerous enough task for an adult fairy to attempt. For a half-human princess who can't control her own magic, it's unthinkable. You'll forgive me, Your Highness, but this is not something you and your lake fairy friend can do together. Leave it to those more powerful and experienced."

"Like you?" Amy asked, planting her fists on her hips and scowling at him.

She wanted to look confident, but his words had stung her. So, she was nothing but a half human who couldn't control her magic after all. Was this how all the fairies saw her?

Cypress coughed into his fist and looked away. "I am not the best choice. Everyone knows I'm Queen Lily's top advisor. If they captured me in the attempt, it would surely lead to war."

"War with who?"

"With whom," Cypress corrected, almost like a reflex.

"The dragons, Amy," Flax answered quietly. "The Tree of Worlds is on Dragon Island."

Cypress nodded at him. He seemed relieved to have a young fairy around who wasn't completely ignorant.

"Fairies are not permitted on Dragon Island. We have a fragile truce with them now, but if we trespass on their land it could re-ignite the dragon war, the war that killed your grandparents."

"Just being caught there at all would start a war?"

"And any fairy who approaches the tree would certainly be caught. Dragons guard it at all times. If I, in particular, were to show my face on Dragon Island, there would be no question that Queen Lily sent me. The dragons would be justified in retaliating." He leaned in with his hands folded behind his back and added in a dark tone, "Dragons would invade our lands within hours."

Amy gulped. She and Flax exchanged a nervous glance.

"So," Cypress said, straightening up and brushing invisible dust from his shoulder. "I clearly cannot go. It would be far too dangerous. It must be a brave, powerful fairy who can believably say the queen did not send them. That is the only chance we have."

## CHAPTER NINE

That night, Amy tossed and turned on her huge fluffy bed. No matter how tight she shut her eyes or how many sheep she counted, she couldn't get to sleep.

She kept thinking about the fairy doors, the things her mother had said in the conference room, and what Cypress had told her. They had to get a piece of wood from the Tree of Worlds. It was so important that the queen had promised to owe an eternal debt to anyone who did it.

Even though it was so important, none of the powerful fairies in the royal court even wanted to try. Maybe they were all afraid that the dragons would catch them. If the dragons figured out that the queen had sent them, it could start a war between the kingdoms. Or maybe they were all hoping someone else would go instead.

Amy kicked off her blanket and slid out of bed, padding through the dim blue light to her window. She closed her eyes and breathed in a deep lungful of cool night air, scented with the sweet fragrance of flowers in the garden below.

Fireflies danced and flashed in the bushes and tall grass around the pond and creek. Glow moss shone with soft blue light in the darkest shadows. The edges of the rippling pond glimmered and sparkled with bioluminescence as water lapped at the shore.

The view was so beautiful, so magical, that it was hard to believe anything was wrong. What danger could threaten a land filled with thousands of magical fairies? But she knew that without enough rowan berries, their magic would run out soon, and fairies couldn't survive without their magic.

Leaning against the windowsill and gazing into the nighttime beauty of the garden, Amy wished she had someone to talk to. If only Flax would show up out of nowhere, like he often did. But he had flown home to Lake Village to help babysit his little brother while his mom made a batch of elixir.

If she knew how to cast spells like a real fairy, she might call up one of the palace's winged horses and go flying. It would be something fun to do, at least. But she wasn't a real fairy. She was a half-human girl who didn't know how to use her magic, just like Cypress had said.

Being without magic in Titania was like being a prisoner, and that wasn't even an exaggeration. When Amy's mother defeated the evil Queen Orchid, they didn't have to lock her up for long. In the end, destroying her talisman so she couldn't use her magic anymore had left her completely harmless. She couldn't destroy fairy doors, enter restricted areas, fight, or do anything dangerous without her magic. She could never be a threat to the throne now. After all, what fairy would listen to a leader who couldn't use her magic?

Amy held her talisman in her palm. It felt warm and comforting against her skin. She ran her thumb over the engraved silver tree, the symbol of the royal family, descendants of the ancient queen Titania.

Would she end up like Orchid someday if she never learned to cast spells the way a fairy queen should? These days, Orchid lived alone in the western wing of the palace. Her magic was enough to keep her alive, but that was about it. It had to be a living nightmare for someone who'd been a powerful queen for so long, who'd known so much about magic spells and could do practically anything she wanted to.

Amy sat up and turned to look through the archway to the empty anteroom outside her chambers, illuminated by the soft blue glow moss in the wall sconces.

Orchid, the former queen, knew the palace better than anyone. Maybe even better than Amy's mother did. What if there was some wood from the Tree of Worlds stashed away in the palace somewhere? When Orchid had been queen, she did everything she could to get rid of all the fairy doors, believing that the human world was too dangerous for fairies to visit anymore. If there was a crucial ingredient to making fairy doors somewhere in the royal palace, she might have hidden it somewhere to keep anyone from using it.

If there was, and if Amy could find it, then nobody would have to go on a dangerous mission to the Tree of Worlds. Nobody would get caught on Dragon Island. Nobody would risk starting another war.

Of course, talking to the former queen, even without her magic, was probably one of those things that Cypress would tell her not to do. So Amy decided she would follow Flax's example. If she went now, before anybody told her not to, she wasn't breaking any rules, was she? Hopefully, her evil aunt would still be awake.

Amy wrapped herself in a silky blue dressing gown, pulled on her slippers, and crept out of her room, heading for the western wing of the palace.

Although Orchid was supposed to be harmless without her magic, Amy still trembled and rubbed her hands together as she made her way through the darkened hallways.

Pale moonlight streamed through the tall windows, painting the floor blue and silver and illuminating the colorful tapestries on the walls.

As Amy drew closer to Orchid's rooms, she could feel magic crackling under the stone floor and up through the walls, powerful spells held in place with intricate runes that glowed and pulsed with faint light. Spells of protection, perhaps. Or maybe they were spells to keep Orchid from trying to hurt anyone or escape. Amy wasn't sure, but she could feel the magic grow more powerful the closer she came to her aunt's chambers.

She rounded one last corner and there it was. At the far end of the hallway, an open archway led into a circular tower room. The pulsing white light of a lantern illuminated it from within.

Humans kept their prisoners behind locked doors and cold metal bars, but for fairies, trapping someone in an enclosed space was too cruel a punishment, even for the worst criminals. Fairies panic when they feel closed in, and trapping someone in a small space is something they'd never dream of doing, even to their worst enemies. When Orchid was queen, she'd put those who fought against her in a prison, but even she hadn't put doors on their cells.

None of the rooms in the palace—or anywhere in Titania—had physical doors or windows. Barrier spells kept bad weather out and fairies or animals from wandering into rooms where they didn't belong.

The arched entrance to Orchid's tower looked like all the others in the palace. It was tall, steepled, and engraved with a series of runes that held the barrier spell in place over the entrance. Amy recognized the tree symbol on the capstone, the same one that was engraved on her talisman. That symbol meant that anyone in the royal bloodline could pass through.

She stopped outside the archway, twisting her fingers together while her heart pounded in her throat. She half hoped her aunt was asleep already. Then she remembered why she came. If Orchid knew where to find magic wood from the Tree of Worlds, they could make new fairy doors. It would mean no one had to go to Dragon Island.

She cleared her throat.

When nothing happened for several minutes, she fidgeted and cleared her throat again, louder this time.

A soft rustling sound came from within, like silk sliding over cushions. Then footsteps tapped over the stone floor and Orchid, the former queen of fairies, stepped into the white light of her lanterns.

Even stripped of her magic, humiliated, and isolated in a corner of the royal palace, the former queen radiated power and a fierce beauty that terrified Amy and sent her heart skipping in her chest.

Orchid no longer wore a royal gown, but the simple green-and-gold dress draped over her frame looked regal, and she still carried herself with authority.

Her dark red hair was a thick halo around her head, probably because she wasn't used to styling it herself and no handmaidens attended her. But even that only made her look more imposing.

Orchid gazed at Amy for a moment through half-lidded eyes, standing tall and proud. Then she seemed to get bored and turned back the way she'd come.

"If you've come to gloat," she said over her shoulder, with no emotion in her voice at all, "please do so quietly. I have more important things to give my attention to than you."

# CHAPTER TEN

Amy scooted closer to the entrance to keep her eyes on her aunt. "Um, no. I didn't come to make fun of you or anything." She paused, gathering her courage. "I have a question to ask you."

Orchid gave a dismissive sniff without looking back. She sat at a wooden desk where a single lantern rested. A dozen glow bugs within hovered and swirled, casting flickering white light over a stack of books.

She lifted a feather quill and dipped it in ink. "Why would I answer any of your questions, halfbreed? Surely your tutors and your mother will tell you everything you want to hear."

"Well, I don't know. I mean, I haven't asked about this because I'm afraid they'll tell me to stop worrying about it. And I don't think they'd ask you themselves, since . . . well, you know." She waved her hand to gesture at the isolated tower where Orchid now lived.

Her aunt turned to look at her with narrow eyes and pursed lips.

"Um, so anyway. What I wanted to ask you is . . . is there some wood from the Tree of Worlds here in the palace somewhere? If you hid some away, we could really use it."

Orchid continued to stare at her. Her chin lifted slowly and the sharp set of her mouth relaxed into a speculative frown.

Amy fidgeted and looked at her feet. She could feel the hot crackle of magic within Orchid. She could also feel that it had nowhere to go, no way to escape. But it still felt dangerous, like a bomb ready to explode.

"This is very interesting," Orchid said finally. "I may have information that would be useful to you. But I wonder, why would the princess be seeking wood from the Tree of Worlds?" She rose from her seat with a flutter of her wings and strode toward the archway.

Amy struggled not to cringe away from her.

"There are many doors to the human world. Lily remembers how to repair them, doesn't she?" A smug smile pulled at the corner of her mouth.

"Well, yeah. I mean, of course she does. I've been helping her. It's just that the Mirror Pool door isn't good anymore. And the door I came through from Grandma

Kerry's house was broken. We need to make more doors, and we need wood from the Tree of Worlds to do that."

Orchid folded her arms in thought for a moment, then shook her head. "There is no reserve of magical wood here in the palace. My sister used the last piece to create the door you came through. But even if I had some, why would I give it to you?" She turned back to her desk and stabbed her quill into the ink pot, then turned to narrow her eyes at Amy. "I have long believed that our reliance on the fairy doors will ultimately doom Titania. We must learn how to survive without them."

"But that's impossible!" Amy yelled. "Fairies were dying without elixir when you destroyed all the doors."

Orchid gestured with her hands in exasperation. "Fairies die going through the fairy doors as well! When too many go through them, humans spot them. It forced them to take risks to avoid detection. And now, with iron tools and machines coming ever closer to the places where the doors lead, the risks grow more every season. We must grow rowan trees here in Titania, where it is safe!"

"Don't you think that they'd grow them here if they could? Flax told me they tried and tried, but it never worked. The trees won't grow here!"

Orchid looked at Amy for a moment with pursed lips. Then she threw her head back and laughed. "Oh, child! My little halfbreed niece. Rowan trees certainly will grow in this realm. I know they will. I can show you proof right now."

Amy balled her hands into fists and clenched her jaw. Orchid seemed to think this was all hilarious, but Amy remembered how pale and weak Flax's baby brother, Acorn, had been without elixir. She remembered seeing the kind old guard, Bromeliad, collapse without his magic. It wasn't funny at all.

"Come closer, child," Orchid said, still smiling. "No, don't be frightened. I won't harm you. I only want to show you something."

Amy hesitantly walked forward through the archway. Like most barriers in the palace, it let her through with no resistance. Even so, she felt a shiver run down her spine as she stepped through the archway and closer to her aunt.

Orchid took a step toward her.

Amy backed up, clasping her talisman in her hand, not sure what magic she could do if her aunt tried to hurt her.

The former queen merely reached out and touched the golden chain that Amy's talisman hung from. "Look at the symbol engraved on your talisman. Think about what it is."

Amy opened her hand, turned the milky white stone over, and looked even though she didn't need to. She already had every root, every branch, and every leaf of the engraved symbol memorized. "It's a tree. It's the symbol of the royal family, descendants of Queen Titania and King Oberon."

"Do you know what tree that is?"

"I . . . I'm not sure. It's a rowan tree, right?"

Orchid nodded and smiled, showing her white teeth. "Yes. It is a very specific rowan tree. It is the Tree of Worlds, which grows in the heart of Dragon Island, in this realm."

Amy blinked and stepped back. "But . . . but I thought they couldn't grow here. How can the Tree of Worlds be a rowan tree?"

"Because they can grow here. Which means we have no need of the fairy doors. Which means your quest to find wood from the Tree of Worlds is pointless." Orchid lowered herself into the seat at her desk and took up her quill again.

"Wait, no! That doesn't change anything! It's not like anyone can go to Dragon Island to collect berries . . . the dragons won't let us go there. We still need to make new doors, at least until someone figures out how to grow a rowan tree in Titania. If you know where some magic wood is, just tell me how to get it. I'll do anything. Just please help me."

Orchid's quill stopped. She set aside the paper she was writing on and closed her book, then turned and arched an elegant eyebrow at Amy. "You'll do anything?"

"I . . ." Amy gulped. Had she really said that? She thought through her words and swallowed hard. She had said that. And she couldn't take it back now.

For a human, making silly promises like that wasn't a big deal. But fairies took oaths very seriously.

When Amy had first met Flax, he'd gotten careless and made a bargain with her, assuming that she was a regular human girl. He'd promised to take her to Princess Lily if she could open a fairy door, believing that she wouldn't be able to. When Amy opened the door, not only was he astonished, but he also had to keep his end of the bargain, whether he liked it or not.

Orchid smiled. "I'm afraid I was telling the truth when I said there are no reserves of magic wood here in the palace. But I will tell you how to get some. I will even offer some vital information that will help you."

Amy licked her lips and swallowed again. Her throat had gone dry. "You will?"

"On Dragon Island, the Tree of Worlds grows in a garden in the center of a ruined city. The tree is guarded day and night by fierce dragons. To get past the dragons, you will need a magical relic."

"Um . . . it kind of sounds like you think I'll be going there," Amy said.

"Of course. You said you would do anything. And

what I demand of you, in return for this information, is that you will bring me living rowan berries from the Tree of Worlds."

"M–me?" Amy's breath started coming fast and shallow. "But I'm only a little girl! I'm not a powerful fairy! I don't even have wings!"

Orchid arched an elegant eyebrow at her with a severe frown. "If you truly believe that, then you're even more foolish than I thought. No mere human girl could wreak as much havoc in this realm as you have."

Amy sputtered and waved her hands vaguely, but she didn't know how to answer that.

Orchid stood over her and spoke in a very serious voice. "Now, are you going to keep your end of the bargain?"

An icy shiver ran up Amy's spine. Goosebumps sprang to her arms and neck. It felt like she was in some mysterious, imminent danger, like an invisible monster was lurking behind her, or like she was standing on the edge of a deep gorge and one wrong step would send her plummeting to her doom. Her stomach twisted, and she felt queasy.

"Um . . . yeah. I will."

The sense of doom passed as mysteriously as it had arrived.

Orchid gave a satisfied smile. "The relic you need is here in Tuleris, in a shop run by a fairy named

Tamarind. He sells magical items and curiosities. Tell him you need the object stored in box three. When he asks for authorization, give him this." She handed Amy a small piece of smooth paper.

Amy took the paper and held it to the light. A silver symbol that looked like an orchid flower shimmered on its surface. "O . . . kay? But how am I supposed to do this? It's supposed to be really dangerous on Dragon Island, right?"

"Yes, it is. For any fairy who approaches the tree without that relic, it is impossible. With it—" she pointed at the paper with the orchid mark "—you might succeed."

The piece of paper trembled in Amy's hand as she gazed at the mark. She couldn't believe this was really happening. It felt like she was walking through a dream. Any moment she would wake up.

"You said you want seeds from the Tree of Worlds. But why? What are you going to do with them?"

"How is that any business of yours?"

"Well, if I bring them to you, whatever you do with them will kind of be my fault, won't it?"

Orchid was quiet for a moment, looking at Amy through narrowed eyes. "Think about it this way. We have been trying to grow rowan trees with seeds from the human world and failing. What might happen if we plant a seed from the tree that already grows here?"

Amy's eyes widened. "Oh! I see. That might work!"

"Do you have any objections to that plan?"

"No. Not really."

"Then it's settled. I expect you to go at your earliest convenience."

NONE of the palace staff noticed Amy shuffling back through the darkened halls in her dressing gown, clutching the piece of paper with Orchid's mark on it. She had to climb up and down several flights of stairs to get to her chambers. She grumbled groggily at the nuisance. Getting around the palace would be so much easier if she could fly.

When she got back to her room, she flopped face-first onto her bed with a groan.

She'd gone to Orchid hoping to find a piece of magic wood to make a new fairy door. Instead, she ended up owing the former queen some kind of magical debt.

What would happen if she backed out of the agreement? Flax had told her about magical contracts before. When she first met him, he agreed to help her if she could open the fairy door for him. He'd run out of magic and couldn't do it himself. When she opened the door, he ended up stuck with the bargain he'd made, much to his annoyance. He'd never said what would happen if he'd tried to break his word.

Amy rolled over and gazed through her window to the night sky. A shooting star flashed through the twinkling blackness.

Did she even want to get out of this bargain?

Everyone said it was dangerous to go to Dragon Island, but she and Flax had done plenty of dangerous things before. No other fairies seemed willing to try. And if the mysterious relic in Tamarind's shop was so important, maybe nobody else could do it even if they tried.

On top of everything, maybe this would finally prove that she belonged in Titania. It would show that she wasn't a pathetic half-human girl who couldn't perform spells. She would be a princess the fairies could be proud of.

# CHAPTER ELEVEN

The next day, Cypress took Amy to the library, where they spent hours with their noses buried in musty books, ancient scrolls, and detailed charts.

According to her tutor, Amy's grasp of runes, geography, and history was severely lacking, so they were taking a break from spell-casting to shore up her other weak points. He assured her it had nothing to do with the rose bush exploding during their last lesson.

Amy wasn't sure whether to be relieved he wasn't asking her to cast spells or to groan at the mountain of books she had to read. Who would have thought reading about fairies and magic could be so boring?

She spent the day learning things like where Piskia, the kingdom of the changelings, was in the west. She found out how far it was from the royal city of Tuleris to the eastern shore where the nereids lived. She even learned which runes held spells in place and which ones would react when touched by magic.

Amy tried not to let her eyes wander to the bottom shelf where the gap in the wall was hidden. She tried not to think about the council meeting that she and Flax had listened in on. But she couldn't forget the worry and determination in her mother's voice when she'd volunteered to go to Dragon Island herself, despite the danger.

It was getting on to evening, and Amy was feeling like the intense studying had replaced her brain with wads of cotton, when Cypress scratched a few notes in his thick notebook, patted the ink dry, and closed it with a loud thump.

"I believe that will do for today, Your Highness," he announced, tucking the book under his arm. "Feel free to frisk about the garden for the remainder of the day. You can practice a few spells while you're at it." He glanced at her sharply. "Nothing major, mind you. Keep your spells small until you learn better control."

Amy nodded solemnly. She had no intention of attempting big spells on her own. Especially not in the garden where anyone could see her make a fool of herself.

She made her way outside and lay in the soft grass by the pond. Tiny fish darted around in the clear water, flitting in and out of the dappled sunlight shining through the branches of the trees. The rippling surface of the pond reminded her of the spell that Flax had shown her—a globe of water that he could hold in his hand.

When Amy had tried it, it had seemed nearly impossible. The water wouldn't listen to her. But then, when she'd gone through the Mirror Pool door, Flax had done something to her and she'd been able to perform spells easily. It had felt like the simplest thing in the world to make her magic do whatever she wanted.

What had Flax done to her? And why didn't it last? Had he somehow given his own ability to her? Or had he temporarily fixed something that was broken inside of her? She'd felt a lot more carefree, more mischievous, more magical. Maybe he'd put the human half of her to sleep somehow.

The palace garden was quiet. Only the gardener fluttered back and forth over the rose bushes by the far ramparts, using his magic to help the foxgloves bloom. It didn't look like anyone was watching her now.

Amy drew her talisman out of her gown, clasping the creamy white stone in her hand. She took a deep breath and placed her other hand, palm down, on the surface of the water, and closed her eyes.

When Flax had done the spell, it had felt like a tiny point of magic hovering over his palm, drawing water around it and holding it in place. Amy remembered the feeling and concentrated, trying to copy it with her own magic.

She lifted her hand slowly and opened her eyes.

A blob of water rose from the surface of the pond, following her trembling fingers. It wobbled and warped as she struggled to focus on the spell despite her pounding heart and tingling excitement.

A rush of wind blew her hair into her face and a shadow flashed over the ground next to her. Someone was there!

Amy gasped and forced her eyes to focus on the blob of water. It wobbled, and she poured a surge of magic into it to keep the trembling mass from falling back into the pool.

The blob exploded, just like Flax's sphere had, just like the rosebush had. One moment it shimmered in the air, and the next moment water flew everywhere, drenching Amy's face and dress and the ground around her.

In the air over her head, someone started laughing.

Amy recognized the voice. She turned her face up and glowered.

"You're getting a lot better at that!" Flax said, not bothering to hide his smirk.

"You distracted me!" Amy stood and started wringing the water out of her hair.

Flax flew lower to hover over the water in front of her. "Sorry about that," he said, still chuckling.

Amy narrowed her eyes at him. "You don't look sorry." She shook out her wet dress and sighed. "But whatever. It was going to explode, anyway."

"Are you done with your studies for the day?" Flax asked, flying closer and dropping to the ground. "Because I've got a great idea for something we can do! Have you ever seen—"

"Hold on!" Amy interrupted. "I have something important to tell you!"

"Yeah?"

"Last night . . . I went to talk to my aunt Orchid."

"You WHAT?" Flax jumped and flew back several feet.

"Don't worry. She's harmless now. Her talisman was destroyed, so she can't do any magic, remember? But I learned some things while I was there."

He still looked worried. "You did? Like what?"

She explained about the relic that Orchid had told her about in Tamarind's shop, and how whoever was going to collect wood from the Tree of Worlds would need it to get past the dragons guarding the gate.

"Oh, and one more thing," she added while Flax rubbed his chin in thought. "I think I made some sort of agreement with her."

He blinked at her and swallowed, wide-eyed. The color drained from his face.

"I don't know if I have to do it or not." She held out her hands to him, hoping to calm him down. "I know you fairies take agreements seriously, but humans usually don't. Will something bad happen if I just stay here and pretend like I never agreed to it? If you break a promise, do you get sick or something?"

"Break . . . a promise?" His voice was hollow with horror and disbelief, like Amy had just suggested eating live kittens.

"Well, I didn't exactly promise. What's the difference between saying you'll do something and making a promise?"

Flax squeezed his eyes shut and shook his head. "What do you mean?" He waved his arms. "There is no difference! For a fairy, our word is binding. Saying you'll do something is a promise! Always! And we can't break our promises. We keep our promises or we die trying!"

Amy gulped and felt her heart skip a beat. "But . . . what happens if you—"

"What did you promise her?" he demanded.

"I don't remember the exact words . . . not everything, anyway."

Flax frowned, looking a lot like Amy's father when he was disappointed.

"I think I agreed to bring her berries from the Tree of Worlds."

"Hold on." Flax held up his hands. "Did you say you would try? Or did you say you would?"

"Does it make a difference?"

"It makes all the difference!" His wings buzzed and he turned away, pacing in a small, agitated circle while he thought.

Amy backed up and realized, with a shock, that she'd never seen her friend truly angry at her before. She'd seen him irritated, sad, frightened, exasperated, in pain, and even in despair. But angry with her? This felt worse than all those things combined.

"Flax, I'm sorry. I thought she'd know where there was some magic wood. I thought if I could find some in Titania, nobody would have to go to Dragon Island. I was begging her to tell me where to find some, so I told her I'd do anything if she'd help me."

"You said you'd do anything?" Flax's voice was incredulous.

"It's just something humans say when we really want something! Then she told me I had to bring her berries from the Tree of Worlds or I'd be going back on my word." She shuddered, remembering the eerie sense of danger she'd felt when Orchid asked her if she was breaking her promise. "If something bad happens to fairies who break promises, maybe it won't happen to me since I'm part human."

Flax stopped pacing and turned to her. "That's true. You aren't a full fairy, but you are magical. I can find out if there is an onus on you. Do you want me to?"

"How?"

Flax glanced around the garden furtively, then grabbed Amy's hand and pulled her under the draping branches of a weeping willow tree. He guided her to the far side of the trunk where nobody would see them, and sat on the leaf-strewn ground.

Amy sat next to him.

"I'll need to take your talisman for a moment. Is that all right?" he asked.

Amy nodded. She wasn't sure what Flax was about to do, but whatever it was, he seemed to be nervous about getting caught. Her heart raced as she drew the golden chain over her head and passed her creamy white talisman to him, feeling a dizzy sense of loss as the talisman left her hands.

Flax took the pendant gently, almost reverently. Then he closed his eyes. His wings relaxed against his back. His own blue talisman glowed against his pale green shirt.

Amy watched in silence, leaning in to see what would happen.

After a minute, her white talisman glowed, shining like silver moonlight in his palms.

Flax opened his eyes and stared at it.

Amy held her breath, watching.

The silver glow flashed red and vanished.

Amy let out her breath and looked at Flax, waiting to hear the verdict.

Flax squeezed the talisman in his fist for a moment and handed it back wordlessly.

"Well? What does it mean?" Amy asked.

"It means you have an onus to abate," he said. "Your word is as binding as ours."

Amy draped the golden chain over her head again and leaned back against the tree trunk. Neither of them said anything for a while. Tiny insects danced in the shafts of sunlight that filtered through the surrounding leaves.

Flax sighed and rubbed his face. "Someone should have warned you. I should have warned you. But who would have thought . . . I mean, any of us would release you if you promised something you couldn't fulfill. But there's no way Orchid will do that."

"Maybe it's not so bad," Amy said.

Flax scooted close to her. "Amy, this is serious. If you don't keep your promise, two things could happen. Either Orchid will set a punishment on you, whatever punishment she wants, or your own magic will turn against you until it drives you mad."

Amy gulped and took a deep breath. "Okay, that sounds pretty bad. But that's not what I meant."

"What did you mean, then?"

Amy sat up straight. "Just think. The Tree of Worlds is a rowan tree. Did you know that? And it's growing on Dragon Island, which is in this realm. If we get seeds from it, maybe they will grow here. Fairies have been trying to grow rowan seeds from the human world, but you haven't been able to try seeds from the Tree of Worlds because you can't go there. What if it's possible?"

Flax bit his lip. "Maybe."

"I can't do spells like a real fairy, but maybe I can do this. I want to prove I'm not just a half-human girl who can't use magic. I want to help."

"Amy, you saved Titania once already!"

"That was mostly you, Flax." She smiled at him. "I couldn't have done anything if you weren't there helping me."

"Why am I feeling more and more nervous about where this conversation is going?"

"I don't want to just sit around in a palace getting pampered and learning boring ancient history and geography and court manners and runes and all that. I want to do something that really helps! Don't you?"

Flax fidgeted as though the roots under his seat were making him uncomfortable.

"And we're not part of the royal court. So if we got caught, there wouldn't be any war because of it. The dragons don't know who I am. I don't even look like a fairy."

"Yeah. But, Amy, this is really dangerous!"

"Will you help me?"

Flax looked away. When he answered, it was quiet and Amy could hear the tears in his voice. "I didn't do a very good job looking after you on the other side of the Mirror Pool door. I'm not a good bodyguard, Amy."

"No! Flax, you were amazing! I don't want a bodyguard with me. I want a friend."

"I am your friend, but I don't think I could fight dragons!"

"I hope we won't have to. But think about it. If someone doesn't do this, there won't be any more rowan berries soon. All the fairies will run out of elixir. You'll all lose your magic again."

His eyes drifted to his feet, and he was quiet for a moment. "Can I think about it?"

Amy sighed and nodded. "Yeah. Sure."

After Flax returned home, Amy was left to spend the rest of the day exploring the garden and the many ornate rooms in the palace.

Her mother and most of the royal advisors were back in the conference room discussing what to do about the broken fairy door and dwindling supply of elixir. The rest of the palace staff went about their business as usual, cleaning and organizing, delivering messages and food, taking inventory of supplies, writing records of events, and making preparations for future gatherings. Whenever one of them saw Amy, they always bowed or curtsied respectfully with a murmured "Your Highness" in greeting.

Amy eventually found herself in the great hall, one of the biggest and most beautiful rooms in the palace. The colorful tapestries on the back wall showed pictures of fairies celebrating all four seasons of the year. Dancing among bright flowers in the spring, harvesting and preserving fruits in the fall, roasting nuts over a warm fire in a snowy winter forest, and playing music on graceful exotic instruments in the summer. Since Amy had come to Titania, she'd never been able to attend the traditional festivities shown. Her mother had been too busy distributing elixir to the fairies who needed it to arrange the seasonal celebrations. And when it seemed they could relax, the two best fairy doors for gathering rowan berries weren't available anymore, and they were back to fighting for survival.

Amy gazed at the picture of dancing fairies in the springtime tapestry. A regal king and queen stood at the head of the group, leading the dance with radiant smiles on their faces. The queen had a silver circlet set in her flowing hair and the king's crown looked like a wreath of golden sage blossoms. Could those be her grandparents? Or maybe they were Queen Titania and King Oberon. Whoever they were, they looked like they were having a lot more fun than her mother ever got to as queen.

A humming noise and a soft breeze got her attention. Amy turned in time to see Flax landing on the colorful mosaic floor. His expression was a lot more serious than it usually was. He stepped toward her with his hands balled into determined fists at his sides.

"Amy . . ." He paused and took a breath.

"Yeah?"

"I've decided. I'll go with you."

# CHAPTER TWELVE

Flax stood in the archway with the light of the setting sun flashing through his splayed wings.

"It's dangerous, more than you realize, but if you have to go, then so will I," he said, his expression solemn and resolute.

"You'll help me? Thank you! I promise I won't—"

Flax held up a hand, cutting her off. "You don't need to promise anything."

"Oh, yeah." She blushed. That was the sort of thing that had gotten her into this mess. "So what made you decide to help after all?"

Flax shrugged and walked across the floor to stand next to her. "Well, I went home for a while. I heard my parents talking about the fairy doors." He stepped closer and looked at the tapestry showing winter fairies roasting nuts over a blazing fire. "They're both worried.

They understand better than most how bad things got when we ran out of elixir." Flax looked at Amy with sad eyes. "I remember too. I remember the fairies who came to my mother for elixir, but she sent them back home because we didn't have any to give. I remember how weak and powerless I felt all the time. I remember the color fading from my mother's wings and my baby brother crying in the night." His voice broke at the end and he went quiet.

Amy didn't know what to say. She reached out a hand and gently rested it on his shoulder.

Flax wiped his arm over his eyes and took a deep breath. "The thought of going to Dragon Island turns my heart to ice," he said.

"Do you think it's hopeless?"

His eyes flashed to hers. "It's never hopeless. Not as long as we have the will to try. I think we could do it, you and I. You look like a human. And if the dragons see me, they won't think I come from the royal palace. We're smaller than the adults, so it'll be easier for us to hide. And we'll have the relic, whatever it is, to help us get past the guard dragons. Maybe it's something that can hide us from all the dragons. Maybe it'll scare them all away from us. We won't know until we try."

"Thank you!" Amy threw her arms around Flax in a tight hug, tears stinging her eyes. Her heart beat wildly in her chest with a mixture of excitement and fear. "I don't think I could go there without you."

Flax nodded and hugged her back. "The sooner we go, the better. We should gather our supplies and leave before anyone catches on and tries to stop us."

THE SHOPS LINING the streets of Tuleris were closing up for the night, the glow in their windows softening and flickering out as fairies covered their lanterns. The sun, sinking lower in the sky, shone in orange-gold rays that washed over the treetops and roofs, glinting like yellow diamonds on the colorful glass windows.

Amy, wearing the simplest light-blue dress in her wardrobe, huddled beneath her traveling cloak as she and Flax stole through the bustling back roads and alleys toward Tamarind's shop.

She felt bad about deceiving her handmaiden, Daisy. She'd told the young fairy that Flax was taking her to the shopping district to look at curiosities and maybe try some fresh pastries, and that they planned to be back after sunset. Hopefully, Daisy wouldn't get in too much trouble when she and Flax didn't come back at all.

Fairies strolled up and down the road in ones and twos or flew overhead on colorful wings, busily finishing their day's activities before the sun set below the treetops of the western forest.

They turned down another stone path. Windows glowed along the trunks of trees. Fireflies danced in the shadows. The smell of warm cinnamon and ginger wafted through the air. Amy kept looking over her shoulder, expecting fairies from the palace to fly down from the sky at any moment and catch them.

"There it is!" Flax said, pointing up the road.

In the base of a wide-branched oak tree, glowing pale light streamed from a narrow archway. The trunk of the oak was far bigger than any tree Amy had seen in the human world, big enough for an entire house to fit inside. Or in this case, a shop filled with magical curiosities.

Half a dozen windows were carved around the trunk at irregular heights and intervals, some circular, some vertical slits, some squares or rectangles. It was as though the owner simply carved a new window wherever he needed more sunlight, without caring how it looked from outside.

Over the entryway, a wooden sign hung with a series of runes that Amy recognized, but she couldn't quite remember what they meant. She made a mental vow to work harder at her rune lessons.

"What does the sign say?" she asked under her breath as they approached the entrance.

"It says, 'Tamarind's Shop of Curiosities and Magical Artifacts.' Kind of a long name, don't you think?"

"Yeah." She studied the runes, trying to make it out for herself. She recognized the word magic, at least. "It looks like a weird shop, but it sounds like this is the right place."

"Oh, it's the right place, all right. Everyone loves Tamarind's shop. He always has the best gag gifts."

They walked through the archway into the store together. A cool musty smell enveloped them, mixed with the scents of spices, old paper, and cedar oil.

All around, shelves upon shelves strained to hold the mountains of intriguing items resting on them.

Amy recognized some items, such as heavy leather-bound books with gold lettering, an hourglass filled with glowing orange sand, quill pens made of long fluffy ostrich feathers, sticks of sealing wax in every color imaginable, and a large goblet made of rainbow-colored crystal. Some items on display baffled her, like a white rose suspended in a jar of clear liquid, a coil of rope that shimmered in the light like it was made of braided gold, or an emerald-green glass bottle that seemed to be filled with liquid smoke.

Amy stepped close to the counter to examine an amazingly lifelike stuffed owl with brown and cream feathers sitting on a perch. She reached out to stroke its soft wings and jumped back when the bird turned its head to blink at her with wide, amber eyes.

"The shop is closing soon. I must ask you to make your selections now or come back tomorrow," a voice called from somewhere in the back of the room.

Flax and Amy exchanged a glance. Flax raised his eyebrows and gestured to her, as though to say, "I'll follow your lead."

Amy cleared her voice. "Excuse me, sir. Are you Tamarind?"

There was a rustling of papers and a scraping sound, like a wooden chair being dragged across the floor. Then a thin old fairy with red and green wings stepped into view from behind a bookcase. He was wiping his spectacles clean with a silk handkerchief. "I am. Is there something I can help you find?" He placed his spectacles on his nose and blinked his blue eyes at her. "Ah! Your Highness. Please forgive me. I did not know I had the honor . . ."

"It's all right." Amy waved her hand dismissively. "I'm, um, actually here to pick something up."

"You are? I'm delighted to help. A magical toy, perhaps? I've got a musical comb that will sing to you as you brush your hair. Or slippers that will make you the best dancer at any party for one night."

"No, I'm not interested in those—"

"Of course not. Of course not!" Tamarind waved his

hands in the air and chuckled. "What am I thinking? You're the crown princess. Only the best will do. Hold on a moment." He turned away and started rummaging on the shelves.

Flax, meanwhile, was browsing around with his hands folded behind him under his wings. He leaned in to peer more closely at something, then grabbed a small box of what looked like blue beans that vibrated and hummed faintly. He held them up and grinned at Amy, as though he were sharing an inside joke with her.

"Ah, here we are!" Tamarind said, catching Amy's attention again. "I have a goblet that will turn plain water into your favorite drink. Almost as good as elixir, eh?" He showed her the rainbow goblet she'd seen on the shelf. Before she could do or say anything, he snatched a deep purple cushion from a basket, brushed some dust off it, and said, "Or how about a cushion that will guarantee only happy dreams if you sleep on it? Stuffed with downy sirin feathers, very precious! Or how about . . ."

Amy held out her hands to stop Tamarind before he could pull a carved wooden stag from a toy box. "Please, I'm here to get whatever is in box three," she said.

He stopped and turned to her. Then he removed his spectacles and started rubbing them clean with his square of silk again. "I . . . I don't know why you would need that particular item, Your Highness. Surely if the queen wished to claim it, she would send . . . um, someone else?"

Amy took a deep breath and squared her shoulders. It seemed like Tamarind didn't think she knew what she was doing. Probably because she didn't. So maybe she needed to look more confident.

"I'm here to claim it. Please get it for me."

"Well . . . I beg your pardon. I just don't know if I can. You see, I'd need proper authorization first. I'm sure Your Highness would rather have one of these . . ." He turned back to the box of wooden toys. They probably had a spell on them that made them prance around like real stags or something.

"Oh, right! I almost forgot," Amy said, reaching into the pouch tied at her waist. "Is this the authorization you need?" She drew out the piece of paper Orchid had given her, with the symbol stamped on it in silver ink. She handed it over to Tamarind and he hesitantly reached out to take it from her, like it made him nervous.

Tamarind gazed from Amy to the mark on the paper. Then he stepped behind the counter and pulled out a looking glass, like the kind jewelers used to grade diamonds. He held it up to his eye and examined Orchid's mark for a few long moments.

When he spoke again, his voice was lower, more serious sounding. "Yes . . . yes, I see. So you have authorization after all. My apologies." He put away the glass, folded the paper, and tucked it into a drawer. "I'll fetch it right away, Your Highness." He bowed low and walked around the corner to the back room.

Flax sidled up to Amy while she stood waiting. "I wonder what it is," he whispered.

Amy shrugged. "He seemed a little scared. Maybe it's dangerous."

"Like a weapon?"

"That would make sense if it's supposed to help us get past dragons. Could it be a dragon-killing sword?"

"Or a powerful charm," he offered. "Or maybe it's a charmed sword."

Amy shivered. "Would it only kill dragons? Or . . ."

Tamarind returned, carrying a long wooden box under his arm. It had a small, tarnished silver plate on the end with a number three stamped on it.

"Here we are," he announced, setting the box on the counter in front of them. "Box three. Let's see, now." He took his spectacles off and rubbed them with his silk cloth again. It seemed to be a nervous habit of his.

Then he drew a wooden tool, like a miniature crowbar, out of a drawer behind the counter and started prying the lid of the box loose. There were no nails keeping it shut, but the wooden pegs set in the lid and sides wedged it so tightly closed that the lid probably had to be hammered on.

Amy and Flax leaned in close to see what was inside.

The lid came away, revealing a mound of yellow, papery, dry moss. Tamarind reached his bony hand in and carefully brought out an ornate cylinder, shivering as his skin touched it. The relic was black like onyx, with bright gold and silver designs that looked like dragons and fire swirling along the length of it.

"It's beautiful," Flax breathed.

"What is it?" Amy asked.

"I thought you would know," Tamarind said, sounding a little surprised. "It is a powerful magical relic, but unfortunately I haven't been able to divine its purpose." He held the object to the light of the glow bugs in the hanging lanterns. The jewels around the top and bottom rims sparkled. "If you press here, something remarkable happens. Careful now." He placed his thumb on a large ruby, and the cylinder sprang into a long and dangerous-looking spear.

Amy jumped back with a gasp, and Flax's wings buzzed in alarm.

"So it is a weapon," Amy said.

"Perhaps. Whatever it is, it is powerful," Tamarind said, pressing the ruby again, and the spear retracted back into itself. "If you hold it, you can feel the magic bursting out of it." His old eyes darted to Amy curiously. "I'm assuming Your Highness can sense magic even though you're half . . . um—"

"Of course she can feel magic!" Flax snapped.

Amy winced. "It's fine, Flax." Then, to Tamarind, "Yes, I can sense magic just like any fairy can."

"Of course, of course. How silly of me." Tamarind chuckled meekly, handing the cylinder to Amy.

The moment it touched her skin, she gasped.

She wasn't sure what the spear was made of, glass or resin or stone or black gold. Whatever it was, it was steeped in magic so powerful it almost vibrated in her hands. It was a kind of magic she'd never felt before. The magic in fairy spells felt warm, exciting, familiar, strong in a way that felt natural to her—like a wave crashing in the ocean, the hot summer sun, or a swift autumn wind.

The magic in the spear felt totally different. The power trapped within it was more like the blast from a white-hot furnace or a jet engine. It wasn't necessarily stronger than fairy magic, but it was a different kind of power altogether.

"What kind of magic is this?" she asked breathlessly. "Who made it? Where did it come from?"

Tamarind leaned over the countertop, resting his elbows on the aged wood, and smiled. "It turns out I am uniquely qualified to answer those questions. My business is learning about magical artifacts—what they do, where they come from, and how old they are." He took his glasses in his hand and rubbed another smudge off a lens before putting them back on. "This relic happens to be ancient indeed. It was made many ages ago, in a land far from Titania, and, I might add, not by fairies at all."

"Do you mean to say that . . ." Flax whispered, gazing at the silver and gold dragon designs decorating the cylinder and the sparkling gems around the rims.

"You can feel it, Your Highness, can't you?" Tamarind asked Amy in a low voice. "The magic in this spear is wild, reckless, and frantic, dangerous even. You know what made that magic."

"Dragons," Amy said without looking up. She knew it. She didn't know how she knew, but she did.

"That's right. This relic is dragon treasure."

## CHAPTER THIRTEEN

The sky was glowing deep blue by the time they left Tamarind's shop. The dragon spear tucked in Amy's bag thrummed with silent magic that she felt sure every fairy they passed was able to sense.

Amy glanced nervously toward the palace. How long would it take for Daisy to realize she wasn't coming back? How long before the palace guards came out searching for them? Would the queen herself come searching for her? Or would she think Amy was out having fun a little later than usual? Did she know a spell that would tell her where Amy was? Did she already know what they were up to? She was the fairy queen! She had to have figured it out already.

Flax led Amy out of Tuleris, taking the smaller roads behind houses and shops where they would be less likely to be noticed.

Amy jumped at every noise, darting glances at all the adult fairies around them. She half expected someone to jump out and grab them from around every corner they turned.

She had told Daisy that they wouldn't return until after sunset, and the sun was only just touching the horizon as they passed through one of the massive gates leading out of Tuleris and made their way along the road.

"We'll need a boat," Flax said. He buzzed into the air and flew backwards in front of Amy as he spoke. "The nearest place to get one is in Luna. Once we have one, we can ride the river all the way out to the sea."

"Isn't Luna farther away from the ocean than Tuleris?" Amy asked, trying to remember her recent geography lessons.

"A little." Flax circled Amy, blowing her hair back with the downdraft from his wings. "But we really need a boat. Dragon Island is too far away to fly without winged beasts. Unless you think you could call Sunblaze or one of the winged horses? They won't listen to me, but you're the princess."

Amy pursed her lips to keep from frowning. "Okay. So we need a boat. Then we'll ride it out to Dragon Island, find the Tree of Worlds, get some wood and seeds, and come back home."

"And not get caught by dragons," Flax reminded her.

Amy shivered. “Right. And not get caught by dragons.”

As the sky faded to a deep red, they met fewer and fewer fairies on the road leading pony carts or flying through the sky on their way home. By the time they came to the river, the sky was nearly black except for a sliver of moon and thousands of twinkling stars. Glow moss grew scattered along the banks, illuminating the rippling water with faint blueish light.

“I think I see a town ahead. Is that Luna?” Amy pointed upstream. Ahead of them, a wide stone bridge stretched over the river. Through the arches underneath, Amy could see a row of white wooden boats moored to a pier with fairy houses along the riverbank and windows glowing in the trees beyond.

“It looks like it,” Flax said. “Stay here. I’ll go check it out. Maybe we can buy a boat at that pier.”

Amy handed him the bag of jewels and herbs that she’d collected to use for trade, and huddled under the bridge to wait for him, wrapped in her dark traveling cloak.

If any fairies at the pier recognized her—which, of course, they would—and realized she was trying to leave Titania, that would be the end of their quest. It was better to let Flax go in and buy a boat himself. He was a lake fairy, after all. Randomly buying a boat would hardly be suspicious for him.

Minutes passed in the dim quiet under the bridge while she waited. She passed the time by pressing her fingers into the glow moss on the stones and watching the soft, squishy stuff brighten under her touch. The blue-white light shone on slender fish in the water, swishing their tails in the current.

Then a heavy, humming noise overhead caught her attention, and she poked her head around the corner of the bridge to see what was going on.

A platoon of ten royal guards was flying into Luna, hovering low over the houses and between the branches of the trees. Their strong wings worked extra hard under the added weight of their armor. Their faces were severe with concentration as they scanned the streets below.

Amy gasped and ducked back under the bridge, curling up as small as she could in her cloak. "They're looking for me," she whispered. "How did they know I was here?"

The guards fanned out into the streets, searching. She could hear the whir of their wings crisscrossing through the town.

Not long after that, a white wooden boat drifted into view over the rippling water with Flax at the tiller. Pale blue light from the glow moss danced against the shallow hull.

"Amy? What's wrong?" Flax asked, guiding the boat

to shore. He hopped out, taking hold of a rope to keep the boat from drifting.

"There are a bunch of palace guards here. I think they're looking for me!"

Flax took a few steps back to get a better view over the bridge. "Oh. Yeah. I see them."

"What are we going to do?"

He raked his hand through his hair. "You could hide in the boat, under the seat. I think there's enough space for you under there."

"But won't they see me?"

"Maybe not, if you wrap yourself in your cloak. You might look like a bundle of supplies." A small frown tugged his mouth. "But it would mean you'd be closed in for a while."

Amy looked at the space under the seat. It was about the size of a dog kennel. Even if she could fit in there, she wouldn't have room to wiggle around at all.

She shook her head. "No, I don't like that. Isn't there something else? Maybe you can help me do magic again. I could make a spell that would get us out of here right away."

He shook his head. "That worked for the humans because they can't sense magic at all. If those guards are looking for you, they'll sense your magic. They'd find you right away if you did a spell like that, especially since you're so powerful."

Amy hesitated, looking at the small space under the seat for a few more moments.

Two of the royal guards turned and started another pass over the town, bringing them closer to the bridge. There wasn't time to think of another plan.

Amy groaned internally and finally let Flax help her aboard.

The little sailboat rocked under her weight. She steadied herself on the mast, then crouched down and crawled under the seat as best she could, tucking in her arms and curling up her legs. Her face was pressed into a dusty corner. Strands of her hair tickled her cheek and nose, but she couldn't even move enough to brush them away.

Flax tucked her robe in around her and everything went dark.

It was stuffy and uncomfortable and cramped. After a couple of seconds, she already felt like she needed to stretch her legs out. The corner of her cloak was bunched up under her nose, making her feel horribly trapped, like someone had tied her up in a sack.

The boat tipped lightly with the sound of the hull scratching against the gravel riverbed. The deep sound of sloshing water came from all around and she could feel the drifting current pull them along.

Amy squirmed, pushing the wooden seat above her with her arm. The hull pressed against her feet, bending them in an awkward angle that was quickly growing uncomfortable.

"Can I come out yet?" she asked.

"Shh!"

She froze, holding her breath. She could hear it now. The distant humming of strong wings was drawing closer. Now it was right overhead. She could feel the downdraft blowing against the outside of her cloak.

Two sets of footsteps landed in the boat, making it rock under the added weight.

"Flax, isn't it? You're Princess Amaryllis' closest companion, are you not?"

Amy recognized the voice, but she couldn't remember the fairy's name. He was one of the castle guards who often stood at the gate.

"That's right," Flax said. "Is everything okay?"

"Nothing to be too concerned about," another voice said. This one Amy knew belonged to Pine, one of her mother's most capable guards and a fierce warrior as well. "The princess told her handmaiden that she was going into town with you, but said she planned to return by sunset. We think she may have gotten sidetracked. Have you seen her recently?"

Amy stifled a gasp. She squeezed her eyes shut and focused on taking small, silent breaths. She didn't want Flax to have to lie for her, but how could he get out of this without lying to the royal guard?

"We did go into town together. I took her to Tamarind's shop. But that was a while ago. Before sunset." His voice sounded worried.

"I see. Well, if you find her—"

"I'll do my best to bring her safely back to the palace," Flax finished for him.

That seemed to satisfy the guards. A moment later, their heavy wings whirred in the air, a gust of wind whipped over Amy's cloak, the boat rocked, and they were gone.

She could hear Flax moving around and tying off ropes, the fabric whipping around as he raised the sail.

Her knees were cramping from being curled up against her chest. Her shoulder was sore from pressing into the wood of the floorboards. Her face felt hot and sweaty from having her breath trapped by the heavy fabric of her cloak. And those infernal strands of hair kept tickling her cheek and nose. She felt like the tiny space was getting smaller and smaller every second, but she didn't dare say anything in case the guards were still watching them.

The boat picked up speed, cutting smoothly through the water. To Amy's great relief, Flax finally pulled the cloak away from her face.

"I think it's safe to come out now," he said.

"Are you sure?"

"We've gone around a couple of bends already. Unless they followed us, I don't think they'll see you."

He took her hand and helped her crawl out of the cramped space under the seat. Amy's legs and arms ached as she stretched them out again. She wobbled as the boat tipped and grabbed the side of the hull to steady herself.

"Thanks, Flax," she said, shakily. "I wonder how they knew to look for me in Luna. Do you think they know what we're doing?"

Flax sat in the back with his hand on the tiller, guiding the little sailboat expertly through the water. He shook his head. "I don't think they knew to look for you there. There are probably guards checking in all the towns around the palace."

Amy bit her lip and glanced back upriver. "How long until we get to the sea?"

Flax shrugged. "I'm not sure. It'll take longer than flying, though. The river moves slower and doesn't go in a straight line. We should be there by midnight, I think."

"Okay." Amy sat on a bench and folded her hands, feeling useless.

They were only taking a boat because she couldn't do spells. If she was a real fairy, she could call Sunblaze or one of the winged horses to carry them. They'd make it to Dragon Island much faster. As it was, she had to sit there and do nothing while Flax steered them slowly downriver.

Amy wrapped herself in her cloak and leaned against the side of the sailboat. The night grew darker and cooler as she watched the water ripple against the smooth hull. The moon and stars drifted overhead, reflected in the shimmering waves. Before she realized what was happening, she slipped into a restless sleep.

# CHAPTER FOURTEEN

The boat lurched and Amy's head bumped into one of the wooden beams.

"Ow!" She sat up, rubbed the sore spot under her messy hair, and blinked around blearily.

The little sailboat was drifting in darkness, surrounded on all sides by open water. Overhead, thousands of stars sparkled in the night sky. The moon drifted low near the distant horizon, casting pale, glimmering light that reflected on the waves, looking like a path leading to the sky.

Water sloshed against the hull, but the sail hung limp from the mast. They weren't going anywhere.

"Flax? What's going on?" she asked, scooting toward the back of the boat.

There was no answer.

"Flax?" She hobbled over the shifting, rocking floorboards until she found him. He was sleeping in the lamplight at the stern, hunched over the tiller.

"Flax!" She shook his shoulder and smacked his cheek gently, trying to wake him.

He took a deep, sleepy breath. "Just ask Acorn," he mumbled. "The pods taste bad." Then a soft snore escaped his mouth.

"What? Flax! Wake up!" She shook him again, a little harder this time.

He shifted, hummed a soft tune, and fell into an even deeper sleep.

Amy huffed and stomped in exasperation. "How could you fall asleep when you're the one steering the boat? You should have asked me to take a turn if you were too tired!"

Something splashed in the water. She peered over the side, trying to see what it was, but the night was so dark over the water she could barely make out anything but the moonlight on the waves and the stars overhead.

She strained her eyes trying to see Dragon Island, hoping the boat was at least aimed in the right direction, but she couldn't see it at all. Not knowing what else to do, she tried pushing the boom aside to catch some wind and get moving again.

Soft humming music caught her attention. At first, she thought it was Flax humming in his sleep again, but this wasn't his voice. It was smoother, more resonant. And the song . . . it sounded beautiful, but eerie and somehow dangerous.

She looked back at Flax. He was resting silently in his seat, leaning against the tiller as limp as a rag doll.

The strange song grew louder, sending shivers up her spine. There was magic in the song. She could feel it shimmering against her, making her eyes heavy.

Moving the boom hadn't worked. The sail hung from the mast without catching even a breath of wind.

Amy scrambled over to Flax and lifted him off the tiller until he dropped to the floor, where he curled up, looking as happy and snug as if he were tucked in bed at home.

A light, musical laugh echoed through the waves, making Amy's breath catch in her throat. The laugh came again, from all around, thrumming through the water and the wood of the boat.

"Who's there?" Amy asked, her voice shaking.

Water sloshed against the side of the boat and Amy peered nervously over.

A face was watching her, bobbing in the waves. As she watched, the face came closer, as smoothly as though it were being carried by a gentle current, not the way she would have expected someone to look if they were swimming.

The face moved into the light of the glowing lantern.

It looked like a girl about Amy's age, only her skin shone with fine blue scales that looked like tiny sapphires. And her hair, thick and reedy like seaweed, was as bright orange as her cat-like eyes.

The strange girl smiled, showing rows of pointed, shark-like teeth.

Amy squeaked in terror and stumbled back, falling into the boat and banging her elbow on the wood.

"What are you doing in my ocean?" the girl asked. Her voice was stern, but it didn't sound scary. It sounded like the voice of a spoiled girl who was used to everyone listening to her.

Amy grumbled and rubbed the bruise on her elbow. "Your ocean? What do you mean?"

Water sloshed again, and the girl rose out of the water to look over the side of the boat. Beautiful blue sapphire scales covered her neck and shoulders. "I mean what I said. This is my ocean. You and this fairy don't belong here."

"How are you doing that?" Amy asked, watching as the girl glided effortlessly through the water without even using her arms.

The girl's strange orange eyes flashed in the lamp-light. "Do what? Swim?"

"It's amazing!"

The girl laughed. "It's easy if you have one of these."

She dove into the water, and a moment later her long, graceful tail broke through the surface and fanned in the air, showing off bright orange fins.

Amy gasped and slapped a hand over her mouth in wonder. "You're a mermaid! I . . . I mean—oh, what did Flax call your people? Nereids, right?"

The girl flipped under the surface and came up again, grinning. "That's right," she said, lifting her chin.

"What's your name? I'm Amy. I've always wanted to meet a mer—a nereid."

The girl looked at her uncertainly for a second before answering. "My name is Nixie. I'm in charge here. You and your fairy friend are intruders. You'll need to come with me for questioning."

"Um . . . but I can't sail this boat myself. I don't know how. And Flax is asleep. I've tried shaking him, but he just won't wake up."

"Of course he won't wake up," Nixie said, rolling her orange eyes. "I sang a spell over him to make him sleep. I don't know why it didn't work on you. Maybe it wasn't strong enough."

"You did that?"

"Of course. It's what we do. Better than making you crash your boat on rocks, don't you think? Of course, you could still crash if everyone's sleeping."

Amy blinked and shook her head, trying to follow

the nereid's train of thought. "But if we're sleeping, how can we come in for questioning?"

Nixie rolled in the waves, sending water sloshing up the side of the boat. "Look, either way, you aren't supposed to be here. Do you think we can just let everyone travel over Naranda? What if you were here to catch all our fish? What if you were trying to steal our treasure?"

"I don't think very many fish would fit in this sailboat," Amy said.

"Well, no. I don't think many fish would fit in your tiny little boat," Nixie agreed, eyeing the boat and frowning thoughtfully.

This nereid didn't strike Amy as the kind of person who was actually an authority. She seemed far too young and unprofessional to be a real guard. Guards in Titania had protocol they followed. If someone suspicious flew into the palace, they wouldn't stand around talking to them and showing off their tail fins, so to speak, like this girl was doing.

In fact, she was pretty sure Nixie was a young girl like her, playing a prank the way fairies often did. Maybe Amy should play along. The nereid seemed more bored than anything else, anyway.

"So, nereids have magic too? That's amazing."

Nixie swam in a lazy circle next to the boat, keeping

her eyes on Amy. "Of course we have magic. You don't know much about us, do you?"

"Well, no. I don't even know much about fairies, even though I'm half fairy myself. I even have magic, I just can't do much with it."

"A fairy girl who can't use magic?" Nixie asked, laughing. "That is funny! How do you know you have magic then?"

"I can use my magic!" Amy said, flushing. "It's just my spells go wrong when I try."

"Really? Show me! I want to see."

Amy hesitated, debating whether to refuse and save her dignity or show the nereid and hope Flax would wake up while she was stalling. Finally, she shrugged.

"Fine, I guess." She held her hand out over the waves, remembering the water spell that Flax showed her. She concentrated, focusing on the pinpoint of magic she needed to form a sphere of water.

When she lifted her hand, a misshapen blob of seawater came up with it.

Nixie watched it with wide-eyed amazement. "Wow, you're doing that all on your own?"

Amy focused harder, trying to get the water to smooth out to a pretty, round sphere like the one Flax had made, but the blob rippled, twisted, and burst into a spray that drenched Amy's hair and dress. She gasped as the cold water soaked through her clothes and dripped from her hair.

Nixie rolled back, splashing the surface of the water with her tail as she burst out in musical, ringing laughter.

"Ugh," Amy grumbled, wringing the seawater from her hair and cloak. "See? It never goes right."

"That was so funny!" Nixie said. "Do it again!"

"What?" Amy stopped wringing water out of her hair and eyed Nixie uncertainly.

"Do it again! That was great!" The nereid's sharp shark-like teeth showed in her brilliant smile. Her eyes sparkled with excitement.

"Well, okay." Amy held her palm over the water again. If there was one thing she knew she could do, it was making a ball of water explode for someone.

To her surprise, it didn't take nearly as much effort this time. The pinpoint of magic formed almost on its own. The spell felt as easy as if someone else was creating it.

She poured more magic in, hoping to draw out more water this time. When she lifted her hand, a huge mass of water rose out of the sea, almost as big as the sailboat she was sitting in. It drifted out, hovering over the waves next to the boat. The new blob of water was as unsteady as before, wobbling all over the place. Here and there, globs fell away, splashing back into the ocean.

Amy stared in amazement and let out an unsteady breath. Her heart stuttered. "I'm doing it!"

Nixie laughed and clapped with delight. "Oh, I have an idea. Watch this!" Then she dove underwater. A second later, the nereid surged back out, leaped into the air, and landed right in the hovering mass of water.

"Whoa! Wait! What are you doing?" Amy cried.

Inside the wobbling water, Nixie swirled around gracefully. Amy could see the bright orange fins on her lithe tail, the drifting tendrils of her hair, and the tiny, bright-blue scales that covered her whole body.

"This is great!" Nixie said. Her voice somehow resonated clearly through the water, without sounding muffled at all. "I can see your whole boat from the top! Hey! What if you could bring water over the land like this? I could even visit Titania!"

Amy trembled, feeling the strain of the spell growing stronger. She tried to focus harder, but she could feel it breaking up, like sand drifting through her fingers. What if she made the water explode again? Would it make Nixie explode, too? How could she live with herself if that happened?

"This has to take a lot of magic," the nereid said as she flicked her tail, spinning within the floating blob. "We nereids use song magic, but it isn't very strong unless a lot of us work together. I wonder if—"

The water burst, falling back to the sea in a tremendous splash that sent a surging wave over the sailboat. A pool of cold seawater sloshed in the floorboards. Flax groaned in his sleep and rolled over.

"Nixie! Are you okay?" Amy leaned over the edge of the boat, searching the depths, but couldn't see a thing. "I'm sorry! I couldn't hold it together!"

The nereid came up laughing and flipped her orange hair out of her eyes. "That was fun!"

Amy shook her head and rubbed her hands over her face. "Okay. I think . . . if you want to take us in for questioning, you should do it now."

Nixie frowned. "Really?"

"I don't want to play with magic anymore. I thought I hurt you."

"But I'm fine! We could play some more."

Amy shook her head. "We're trying to get to Dragon Island. I can't stay out here playing all night. So you'd better take us to your queen or king or whoever so they can ask us their questions."

Nixie arched an eyebrow. "Hmm, you really don't know very much about us, do you? Are you really going to Dragon Island?"

"Yes, we have to. That's where the Tree of Worlds is, and we need to collect some wood from it."

"You're not here to steal fish?"

"No! Of course not."

"And you don't want to take our treasure?"

"Why would I want your treasure?"

Nixie pursed her lips and scowled in disapproval.

"No! I don't want your treasure! I didn't even know nereids had treasure." Amy waved her hands and huffed out a breath. "We're just trying to get to Dragon Island."

"Well, in that case . . ." Nixie swam in a slow circle next to the boat. Her hair streamed out behind her. Her tail broke through the surface, sparkling blue in the moonlight. "I've been thinking. Maybe I'm okay with you and your friend being on my ocean."

Amy sloshed through the shallow water in the boat, following Nixie as she swam. "You are?"

"Yes. So, if you want to come back to play some other time, I guess you can."

"Well, that's nice of you."

"It is, isn't it? I'm a very nice person." Nixie grinned, flashing her sharp teeth again. "In the meantime, I suppose we can help you get where you're going."

Before Amy had a chance to ask what she meant, Nixie dipped below the waves again, splashing the surface with her tail fin.

"Wait. You'll help us? What do you mean? How?" She leaned over the side, searching for any sign of the nereid.

From the depths of the sea, all around the little sailboat, the water started pulsing with greenish-blue light.

Amy watched in fascination as dark forms swirled in

the glow as it brightened and dimmed in a slow rhythm. The forms grew larger, taking the shapes of long-tailed mer-folk as hundreds of them swam in a wide circle around the boat, growing closer to the surface every moment.

"Wow," she breathed.

The glow brightened, illuminating the white hull of the sailboat from below, shining bright green on the sail and mast. The boat turned slowly in the water as the current swirled around it.

Then she heard the singing. It was faint at first, but grew in volume as the nereids rose to the surface. The louder the song grew, the faster the water moved, and in a few moments, the sailboat was rushing forward in a swift current.

A rich, merry melody danced along the waves as the mer-folk sang, filling the air with joy. Now and then, a laughing nereid jumped from the glowing current like a dolphin, splashing back in and jumping again moments later. Hundreds of them—men, women, and children—followed along, singing and laughing, combining their magic to create a rapid current that carried the boat along.

Holding tight to the bow, Amy suddenly realized that Nixie hadn't been bluffing. She may look and act like a child, but when she said this was her ocean, she'd been telling the truth. She must be an important person in the sea kingdom for all these other nereids to listen to her.

The music swelled in the waves, growing slower, deeper, and more soothing as they traveled.

Amy's eyes felt heavy. She rested her head against the gunwale and relaxed against the rocking motion of the water. Cool wind blew over her face as the boat rushed ahead and the song continued.

# CHAPTER FIFTEEN

"Amy! Amy, wake up!"

Hands grabbed Amy's shoulders, shaking her gently and snapping her out of a deep sleep.

She groaned and rolled over. Her head throbbed and her neck ached where she'd been resting against the side of the boat.

She blinked the sleep out of her eyes and saw the white sail of their boat rippling overhead in a choppy wind. The boat wasn't rocking under her anymore, and the crashing sound of waves breaking over rocks filled her ears.

She sat up and the motion made her head spin. "Where are we?"

Flax crouched next to her and ran his hand through his hair, looking bewildered. "I think we're on Dragon

Island. I don't have a clue how we got here. I can't believe I fell asleep! Did you steer us here?"

Amy blinked and looked out at the wide blue ocean, half expecting to see mer-people swirling and leaping in the waves. Strange images filled her mind like déjà vu, but the harder she tried to remember them, the further away they drifted: glowing green water, sparkling blue scales, and a haunting melody that made her feel like lying down and falling asleep. It must have been a weird dream caused by sleeping on the deck of a rocking boat.

She swallowed and shook her head. Her mouth and throat felt dry. The skin of her face was tight and scratchy from the salty spray. "I think the current must have carried us here. Are you sure we're on Dragon Island?"

"It looks like it. What other island would be so scorched and barren?" He turned and waved toward the land with a disgusted frown.

Amy looked. The waves had carried them up to a rocky shoreline rimmed with short, scraggly bushes. They seemed to be completely alone. The island appeared uninhabited. No animals scurried past. No birds flew in the air. Scarcely any insects even buzzed around them. The only trees that grew were short, thin, spindly things that looked like they'd only been alive for a season or two. The air smelled faintly of ash and smoke. Blackened soil, filled with charred bits of wood and gray ash, covered the ground.

Over a distant hill, Amy caught a flash of light glinting off the wings of a massive creature with a long, spiky tail. A thin trail of smoke followed as it spiraled down to land.

"Is that . . . a dragon?" she gasped.

"I think it is," Flax said. "I hope it doesn't see us."

They watched together with bated breath until the flying dragon descended out of view.

"Okay. We need to get out of here," Flax said. "It would be too easy for a dragon to spot us in the open like this."

They jumped out of the boat and Amy helped Flax hide it under a mass of dead-looking bushes and thorns. It took a long time. Even though the sailboat was small and the mast could fold down flat to the deck, they had to push a lot of bushes and shrubs around it before it couldn't be seen anymore.

With the boat hidden, they went farther ashore and found a concealed clearing under the scraggly trees where Flax dug a hollow in the dirt and used magic to draw water from the ground.

Amy watched in amazement. "Is that the same water spell you used on the pond?"

He nodded with a wry grin. "I never knew it would

come in so handy. In a horrible place like this, it might be the only fresh water we can find."

Amy nodded appreciatively, wondering if she'd ever be as good at magic as he was.

An image of a huge blob of water exploding and splashing into the ocean flashed in her mind. She blinked and shook her head.

"I think I had some weird dreams last night," she said.

Flax chuckled. "Yeah, me too. I dreamed Acorn wanted to eat stink pods. When I wouldn't let him, he sang a song mocking me."

Amy laughed. "I think I heard you talking about that in your sleep!"

They refilled their water jugs and took turns bending down to drink from the clear water before Flax released his spell.

"Now we have to figure out where to go," Flax said. He brushed his hands together and looked around speculatively.

"I brought a map," Amy said, unbuttoning the bag strapped to her hip. "I found it in the palace library. Here." The magic dragon spear glinted from within the bag as she pulled out a rolled sheet of thick paper.

She laid the paper on the ground and spread it out. The map of Dragon Island was old. She wasn't sure how old, but the paper was yellowed and worn at the edges. Time had faded the ink in places.

"There's the Tree of Worlds," Flax said, pointing out the artfully designed tree in the middle of the island.

"Yeah. But I can't read these words." Amy pointed to a few dots scattered around the map, each labeled with tiny artful runes. "What are they?"

"Maybe dragon villages? Or places where battles happened? This one here says Scorched Earth, that one says Drifting Ash, and this one here says Field of Doom." He winced and rubbed a hand over his face. "Maybe it makes better sense to the dragons."

"If dragons live there, we should try to avoid those places," Amy said with a frown.

"I completely agree," Flax said, nodding.

"So if we start walking and stay away from those places, maybe the dragons won't even notice we're here."

"That would be nice, but I have a feeling they'll notice us no matter what, unless we find good places to hide," Flax said.

"Well, do you have a better idea?"

Flax sighed, rolled his eyes, and said with a touch of irritation in his voice, "The smart thing to do would be to figure out where we are on the island first. Then we could figure out how to get to the Tree of Worlds. We can find good hiding places along the way."

Amy narrowed her eyes at him. "All right, Mister

Smarty-Pants. Do you want to figure out which part of the island we landed on then?" She pushed the map toward him.

Flax sighed and rubbed his face with his hands. "I'm sorry. I don't mean to be bossy. It's just, being here makes me nervous."

They studied the map together, comparing the coastline and hills surrounding them with the ones displayed on the map. They debated back and forth over where they were on the coast, both of them arguing that they could be practically anywhere on the outside of the talon-like peninsulas.

In the end, they finally agreed that they should go inland and bear a little left. The Tree of Worlds grew at the top of the tallest hill on Dragon Island, in the "palm" of the dragon claw. If all else failed, they just had to keep going uphill. At least, that's what they told themselves.

Despite Flax's nerves, Amy felt better having some sort of plan, even if it was hastily made. She took a deep breath, trying to relax, then rolled the map back up and tucked it into her bag.

"All right." She stood, brushing ash and dust from her dress. "Then I guess we just start walking."

Flax stood, too. He shrugged and nodded agreement, but his wings buzzed nervously a few times. "I guess so."

They turned away from the ocean and marched inland, heading into the shrub-covered hills.

They checked the map from time to time, never sure whether they were going the right way. The way Dragon Island was shaped, if they'd landed on the outside of a peninsula, they could end up at another shoreline soon. If that happened, they'd have to choose whether to turn right or left. But, not knowing where they were to start with, making the wrong choice would mean they'd be going in the opposite direction from the Tree of Worlds.

Flax assured her that if they got up high enough, they could see more of the island, recognize some landmarks, and figure out which way to go from there. So they trudged on, stopping only to eat some honey cakes and drink water, while the sun silently glared down on them from the sky.

Hours passed. Amy's legs felt rubbery and weak. The daylight was shifting from pale blue to red and orange when they finally crested a tall hill. Below them, a smooth lake reflected the fiery orange sky. Surrounding the lake, clusters of short, bushy trees grew.

Amy's feet and legs throbbed from walking so far. Sweat was beading on her forehead. Her throat felt like she'd swallowed a mouthful of sand, and her cheeks felt like they were on fire. "The sun's going down. Do you think we should rest here overnight?" she asked, trying to sound like she could go on for hours still if they needed to.

Flax took a deep breath and stretched his shoulders

and back. Then he wiped his arm over his brow. "Yeah, I guess so. Looks like a pretty good place to hide."

They descended the slope, Flax hopping lightly over roots and stones and Amy stumbling on her tired wobbly legs. When they reached the bottom, they made their way to a clump of small trees near the lakeshore and curled up in the thicket that would hide them through the night.

Roots poked out all over from the hard, rocky ground, completely different from the soft, thick moss and delicate flowers in Titania. But Amy was so tired it hardly mattered anymore.

"So, tomorrow we'll figure out which way to go from here," Amy said as the last of the light faded. She curled up and tried to shift some of the sharper rocks out of the way.

"That sounds like a good plan," Flax agreed wearily.

"Do you think this will work? Do you think we'll make it all the way to the Tree of Worlds?"

Dry grass and leaves crackled as he shrugged his shoulders in the dark. "I think it's possible. I know it's dangerous, but we have to try."

Amy bit her lip and felt her eyes fill with unshed tears. Flax was a good friend for coming with her. If they got caught, it would be all her fault. She might have made a silly mistake when she promised to get berries from the Tree of Worlds for Orchid, but Flax hadn't made any silly promises. She was the one who had asked him to come along. He should have stayed home, where it was safe. Only she wasn't sure how she'd do any of this without him.

As she lay there in the dark thicket, she tried to tell him he could go home. She opened her mouth to say the words several times, but she couldn't get them to come out, no matter how hard she tried.

Finally, with the sound of water gently lapping at the lakeshore and the stars glimmering faintly overhead, she drifted into a restless sleep.

A GUST of wind whipped through the spiky tree branches, showering Amy with a spray of dewdrops and dead leaves.

She squeezed her eyes shut and clenched her teeth, shifting her back to find a more comfortable position. An annoying little root that poked out of the ground had spent the entire night trying to dig into her spine, no matter how she rolled over to avoid it.

A heavy thump shook the ground and made her eyes blink open in confusion.

She tried to sit up, but the surrounding bushes were so thick that she kept getting scratched and poked. A second rush of wind rustled the branches and leaves, sending them scratching and scraping against her cheeks and hands as she struggled to see what was going on.

"Flax? Flax!" she called, looking around. The little thicket was empty, except for herself. She saw the hollow in the earth where her friend had been sleeping, but he was gone.

Another shuddering thump on the ground grabbed her attention, and she whipped her eyes around to the twilit lake.

When she saw what was out there, her heart jumped, stuttered, and started beating double time.

It was dragons!

# CHAPTER SIXTEEN

Beyond the bushes, the world was mostly gray. The overcast sky overhead varied in cottony gray shades. The water of the smooth lake reflected the gray clouds like a mirror. The ground, full of ash and charred wood, was a gray so dark it was almost black. Even the stubby trees and prickly bushes spread twigs, thorns, and leaves in shades of gray with only hints of green.

So when Amy's eyes fell on two bright spots of color, she noticed them right away.

Down by the lake, two huge, winged forms stood. Their scales shone with such vibrant clear colors they might as well have been made of jewels. One was a copper color so bright it looked almost gold. The other was a deep red that blended into green along its crest and wingtips.

"Dragons!" Amy breathed, trembling.

She had to hide. She knew she had to do everything possible to keep the dragons from finding her where she cowered in the bushes. She should drop to the ground and bury herself under as much bracken and shrubbery as possible. Even though she told herself these things, and it seemed like a very good idea, she couldn't make herself move. She stood, frozen in place with fear, watching the beautiful dragons pace the water's edge.

Where was Flax? He must have left their thicket while she was sleeping. Why didn't he wake her to tell her where he was going? Did the dragons catch him already? Did they eat him? Were they here now looking for her?

She started trembling harder and felt tears prickling in her eyes.

"All the good fish are gone from the lake," the red dragon growled.

Amy held her breath and cocked her head to the side. Had that dragon actually spoken?

No. Not really. The dragons weren't speaking English or any human language at all. The sounds she'd heard were growls, snarls, and snorts.

Somehow, though, she'd understood what the dragon had said as clearly as if it was talking with a human voice. Some sort of magic must have made it possible.

"It's a big lake," the copper dragon said. It ruffled its leathery wings, revealing greenish-gold colors underneath. "And we're here early enough, there might still be something worth catching."

The red dragon snorted, sending up a puff of greasy black smoke from its nose. "This is a waste of time. We should be fishing out in the ocean."

The copper dragon grumbled something unintelligible as it paced along the water, lashing its spiky tail like an angry cat.

The pacing drew it closer to Amy's hiding spot.

Terror finally made Amy's muscles unfreeze. She scrambled back, trying to hide deeper in the branches. Her foot slipped and a twig snapped. The broken edge sprang up, adding a fresh bleeding scratch to her leg.

The copper dragon stopped pacing and swiveled its head toward her. "What was that?"

"I said that we should be fishing in the ocean! Even if most of the others will be serving ocean fish, we can use my spices to make ours stand out," the red dragon grumbled, rolling its eyes.

"Not you!" the copper dragon snapped, turning its head to glare at the red dragon. Then it stared into the bushes near Amy's thicket. "I heard something. There might be an animal hiding in there."

"Oh!" The red dragon lumbered closer. "Something

else we can prepare for the festival? Something other than fish?"

The copper dragon snuffled the air and rumbled appreciatively. "What is that smell? I don't recognize it. Whatever it is, it smells . . ." It licked its chops. "Mmm . . . delicious."

The red dragon sniffed, too. "It smells almost like a human. Move carefully, we can't frighten it away."

The dragons crept closer, sniffing the air as they went.

Amy held her breath and crouched down as small as she could make herself.

"It can't be a human," the copper dragon whispered, slithering its head through some of the trees right over Amy. "That's impossible. No human could come here."

"I don't care what it is, as long as it tastes as delicious as it smells!" the red dragon said.

"But if it is a human, maybe it's dangerous. It may have a sword or a spear."

The red dragon snorted, sending a cloud of choking smoke right into the thicket where Amy cowered. "Myths and legends! Don't believe those old stories. Sure, maybe one or two humans got lucky in days gone by. And just think! If it is a human, we would be sure to win us the treasure at the summer fair!"

They were so close now that Amy could smell the

musty scent of their scales. She could feel the heat radiating from the fire in their bellies.

She tried to use the hiding spell that Flax had shown her in the crystal cavern, but she couldn't do it. She couldn't stop trembling long enough to even start. She tried bundling her magic into a blast of energy to fire at the huge beasts, but she couldn't control it. She couldn't keep hold of her magic at all. It kept slipping away like water through sand. She couldn't do any spells at all. The dragons were going to eat her and she couldn't do anything about it!

Just then, a shrill whistle came from the trees on the far side of the dragons.

The dragons snorted, lifted their heads, and snaked their necks around to look.

"Hey, scaly snoots! I bet you can't catch me!"

Amy slapped her hands over her mouth to keep from shouting in surprise.

From the short trees on the other side of the bank, Flax flew out, holding his fists against his hips like Peter Pan. His translucent wings flashed and buzzed in the pale gray light. A few twigs and leaves clung to his tousled hair and clothes. He grinned at the dragons and flipped playfully in the air, like he didn't have a care in the world.

The dragons snarled and bared their sharp teeth.

"A fairy!" the copper dragon roared, letting out a wisp of flame.

"Kill it!" the red dragon bellowed. It spun in place and lurched out of the trees toward Flax.

Both dragons whomped heavily over the rocky bank, while Flax flew in a mocking figure eight above the trees, whistling and laughing.

"What is he doing?" Amy gasped, unable to look away. He was going to get himself killed if he kept that up!

"Hey, I didn't know dragons could run backwards!" Flax called. "Oh, wait. Sorry! Those are your faces. I thought they were your rear ends!"

The red dragon was so furious it seemed to choke on its own smoke.

The copper dragon reared back and blew out a massive gout of flame, singing the trees. Flax buzzed out of the way just in time.

"Is that the best you've got? I should have brought some chestnuts to roast."

"You'll regret this, you stinking, filthy fairy!" the red dragon roared. It lurched to its hind legs and leaped into the air, beating down with its massive wings. The copper dragon followed immediately after, and together they flapped into the air, circling upward and puffing out clouds of smoke.

Flax flew higher but didn't seem to be trying very hard to get away. He let the dragons catch up to him, circling, snapping with their jaws, and blasting with bursts of flame. He darted back and forth, avoiding the searing blaze of dragon fire, swiping claws, and biting teeth.

Try as they might, the dragons couldn't seem to maneuver fast enough to catch him.

Amy watched, feeling useless as her friend danced around, narrowly escaping the dragons in the air.

Finally, Flax darted up and laughed. "Ha! You call that flying? This is flying!" He zoomed out of reach again and darted away, leaving a trail of sparkling magic in his wake.

"Don't let him escape!" the red dragon snarled.

At the same time, the copper dragon roared, "Get back here, stinking fairy!"

And they were off, chasing after Flax, picking up speed as they gained altitude.

"Oh no . . ." Amy murmured. "They'll catch him for sure. What'll I do? I have to save him!" She grabbed her bag, stood, and felt something thump against her foot. It was the dragon spear. It must have wiggled out of her bag sometime during the night while she tossed and turned.

She reached down and took it in her trembling hand, feeling the surge of terrifying magic within.

A sudden crash behind her made her whirl around in alarm.

Without thinking, she tried stabbing whatever it was with the spear. Since it was still retracted into a cylinder, she only managed to smack something with the flat dull end.

"Ow! What did you do that for?"

"Flax?"

It was Flax, panting heavily, drenched in sweat, looking pale and weak, and rubbing his chest where she'd thumped him.

"Flax! Thank goodness you're all right!" She threw her arms around him in a tight hug. Even sweaty, he smelled like a grassy meadow the morning after a storm.

Flax chuckled weakly and took a deep breath, hugging her back. "Yeah, barely all right. I don't think I could do that again. Those dragons almost got me a few times."

He grabbed her shoulders and pushed her back, furrowing his brow. "What are you still doing here? I was distracting them so you could escape! Come on, we have to get out of here before they come back!"

"Oh. Right!" She stuffed the spear back into her bag and followed Flax out of the thicket and away from the lake.

The going was more difficult than it had been the

previous day. Now that they'd seen dragons, they wanted to stay hidden under the cover of trees. They couldn't stay in the thickest cover either, because the dense vegetation made it impossible to walk without making a lot of noise.

They ended up dashing for cover through open areas, pausing to check for danger, and then making a dash for the next safe place they could find. They constantly searched the sky for wisps of dragon smoke or glinting scales. In this way, they slowly made progress toward the next big hill on the horizon. Amy wondered if this was what life was like for mice and rabbits, constantly watching the sky for hawks that might swoop in and eat them.

As they ran, Amy noticed that Flax was looking kind of pale. The colors flashing in his wings weren't as bright as they used to be, and he had slight shadows under his eyes.

"Flax?" she said.

He glanced at her.

"Are you all right? Do you need some elixir?"

He pressed his lips together, like he was trying not to grimace. "I'll be okay. That stunt with the dragons took a lot of magic, that's all."

"You were amazing! I almost couldn't keep from laughing the whole time!"

He smirked. "Getting them too angry to think

straight seemed like my best bet. I read it was a common strategy in the dragon war."

"Really? No wonder the dragons hate fairies so much," she giggled.

He snorted. "Yeah. That makes sense. Imagine getting your tail whipped by a puny creature that keeps mocking you the whole time!"

They both laughed.

"But really," she pressed. "We brought an extra vial of elixir for you. Maybe you should drink some of it now."

He sighed. "The truth is . . . I already did."

"What?"

He winced. "I drank it all a little before facing the dragons." He looked at her and hurried on. "I knew I was going to use a lot of magic. I had to confuse them so they couldn't hit me. And I needed a boost so I could out-fly them and get back before they turned around."

"But that was all the elixir we had!"

"I know!"

"It was supposed to last us a month!"

"I know!" He raked his hands over his face and growled in frustration.

"And we don't know how to make more!"

"Amy, I know!"

They were both quiet for a while.

Amy looked at her feet and sighed. "I know you only

used it up because you were saving me from those dragons. It's just . . ."

Flax folded his arms. "I know." He chuckled and sighed. "I still have some magic left. If I don't have to work too many big spells, I should make it to the Tree of Worlds. Just don't let any more dragons try to eat you, and we'll be fine!"

Amy shot him a look that was half smirk and half glower, and together they ran to the next cluster of trees.

She couldn't stop thinking about what it meant, though. If Flax ran out of magic, they didn't have any more elixir for him to drink. He wouldn't be able to replenish his magic until they got back to Titania.

She wasn't nearly as mad at Flax as she was with herself. He was doing what he had to do to keep them alive. But if she could use her magic like a fairy princess should, he wouldn't have had to save her in the first place!

How much of his magic had he used? Half? More than half? If they got in trouble again, would he have enough to save them? They'd only just gotten to Dragon Island, and already it looked like they wouldn't make it to the tree.

# CHAPTER SEVENTEEN

"It isn't your fault, Amy," Flax said. "I'm the one who drank all the elixir. And I'm the one who used my magic on a bunch of flashy spells."

They'd walked all morning through hills of prickly bushes and sparse trees. As the day wore on, the hills gave way to barren, rocky fields strewn with enormous boulders and short, scratchy grasses that hardly seemed alive. Now and then, a gust of wind or distant rumbling sound sent them scurrying for the shelter of the nearest boulder. Despite their constant looming fear, the landscape seemed abandoned.

"If I could use my magic the way I should, you wouldn't have had to do all those spells!" Amy countered.

"You can do spells! If you believe in yourself and keep practicing—"

"I've been practicing!" She scoffed and shook her head to hide the tears welling in her eyes. "It just doesn't work. Maybe I helped you defeat Queen Orchid, but that doesn't make me a real fairy princess. I can't do all the things you can. I'm still half human."

"You're also half fairy," Flax said, hopping over a blackened stone and landing in a patch of crunchy grass. He frowned at the withered vegetation for a moment, then continued. "And not just any fairy, either. Your mother is Queen Lily, the most powerful fairy in Titania. Don't forget that."

Amy bit her lip and kicked a little lump of charred wood out of their path.

Queen Lily was powerful. Amy had seen her do things with her magic that no other fairy could come close to. When the throne room of the palace had been destroyed in a battle, her mother used her magic to repair the damage as easily as if it were a sand castle. This was after she'd already cast several other powerful spells to conceal her warriors, fight in the battle, and bind her wicked sister in an enchanted sleep. After all that, she'd still had enough power left over to heal her injured soldiers after the fighting was over. It seemed like there was nothing she couldn't do if she wanted to.

What was her mother doing now? When the royal guard had returned without Amy that night, did she guess what they were up to? Did she know where she and Flax had gone? Did she tell Amy's dad they'd run away to an island full of murderous dragons?

The farther they walked in the dry, desolate landscape, the more Amy felt sorry they'd come at all, but it was too late to turn back now.

Eventually, the rocky plains gave way to fields of dark-green, close-cropped grass. Now and then they spotted herds of animals—cows, sheep, goats, even pigs—all contained behind walls of heavy stone.

It was a relief to see something green finally, even if it was a dull, sickly green. Until then, it had seemed that Dragon Island was nothing but a pile of burned wood and volcanic ash.

Seeing the grass, the walls, and the animals gave Amy a sense of unease. Those animals were obviously there on purpose, contained behind rocky walls in grazing fields. These were food animals, and that meant dragons lived nearby to tend to them.

Amy and Flax stopped now and then to munch on a few bites of honey biscuits. The biscuits were dense, sweet, a little sticky, and reminded Amy of eating the buttercream frosting off of cupcakes.

The fairies made them as traveling food for berry gatherers. When fairies had to journey far from fairy doors in search of rowan berries, they needed food that would last a long time and give them plenty of energy. But that didn't mean they would last forever.

By the second morning, Flax drew the last two biscuits out of his bag and handed one to Amy with a grave expression.

"Well, I guess we need to find more food," Amy said, taking the biscuit with a shrug.

Flax's expression shifted to a wry smile, and he gave a nervous little chuckle. "I was kind of getting sick of honey biscuits, anyway."

"You think we could find something to eat around here?" Amy scanned the grassy fields with her eyes. A small herd of shaggy brown cattle grazed in the distance, swinging their tails lazily as they ate.

Flax snorted. "In this miserable place? These stupid dragons hardly let anything grow. There aren't any berries, or nuts, or mushrooms, or edible roots at all. They've burned everything but the grass for their cattle."

"But there is the grass."

"Not even fairies can eat this grass," Flax grumbled around a mouthful of biscuit, glaring at the gray-green fields.

"No, but the animals do. I bet that's why they burned down all the trees, to make more room for grass to grow. Maybe, if we had to, we could steal some of their meat."

Flax made a disgusted expression. "Ugh. Meat. Nasty stuff."

Amy blinked. "Don't fairies eat meat?"

"No, of course not!"

She stared at him, trying to remember all the things she'd eaten in Titania: berries, nuts, vegetables, roots, beans, herbal teas, candies, hundreds of fresh fruits, bread, soup, and lots of milk and cheese dishes. How had she never noticed the absence of meat before?

"Not that I think less of you for eating it, though," Flax added hurriedly. "I mean, it's only natural for you."

Amy gave him a look and stood, brushing the dust from her skirt. "You mean because I'm a human?"

"Well, yes, I mean, sort of . . . you're part human. Humans have always eaten meat. Well, most of them do." He shrugged.

"Never mind." She sighed, letting it go. "What this means is that we'll need to find food soon or we might starve."

Flax nodded, but his brow furrowed with doubt.

For the rest of the day, as they walked, they scoured the underbrush and sparse shrubbery, searching for anything that looked remotely edible.

Flax found a bush with dry spiky seed balls growing all over it. When he tried to eat one, the spikes dug into his fingers and they had to spend an hour pulling all the tiny prongs out of his skin.

Later, Amy lifted a rock to find a bright orange lizard with white and black star markings along its back. As she was leaning over it, wondering how a lizard would taste if they roasted it over a fire, Flax came up and yanked her away. "Don't touch it!" he yelled, pulling her back as far as he could.

"Why? It's just a—"

"It's a salamander! They're poisonous, and if you make one mad, they can spit fire at you that will keep burning even if you dive into water."

"Oh." Amy backed away, eyeing the salamander nervously.

The creature cocked its head at her, flashed its tongue out to lick its black eyeball, and scurried away.

Flax sighed in relief and they kept going.

They still had found nothing to eat by the time the sun was sinking toward the horizon again. Not wanting to get caught out in the dark, they settled in for the night in a gap between two large boulders.

Amy's stomach rumbled and ached with hunger as she tried to find a comfortable position on the rocky ground.

The smell of smoke, which lingered everywhere on Dragon Island, made her think of summer barbecues with her dad. She pulled in a deep breath through her nose. Was it her imagination or did it smell like cheeseburgers, pork ribs, and grilled salmon?

She inhaled another breath, sniffing at the delicious, smoky wind. Her stomach twisted and her mouth watered.

"Why are you doing that?" Flax asked sleepily.

"Don't you smell that?"

Flax sat up and sniffed the wind experimentally. "Smoke? It smells like smoke everywhere here."

"No . . ." She sniffed again, then crawled out of their little shelter, looking around for the source of the smell. "It smells like food!"

"What do you mean? I don't smell food."

Amy started walking up the rocky slope and Flax scrambled to follow her, buzzing his wings to keep up. The sun was so low it was hard to look ahead, but Amy kept going, sniffing the wind as she went.

She knew it was a silly thing to do. What was she expecting to find, a long table with a checkered tablecloth piled with plates of barbecued food? But she was so hungry, she had to find what made that delicious smell.

She scrambled to the top of the hill, blinking in the bright sunlight.

Flax sprang up beside her.

A low cloud drifted in front of the setting sun, blocking the glare and clearing their vision so they could see what lay before them in the valley.

Amy gasped.

Flax yelped in alarm.

Immediately, they both dove for cover by the nearest craggy boulder.

Below them, on the far side of the hill, the land swooped down into a low flat valley that stretched for miles.

On the far side of the valley, hazy in the distance, the land rose into a green hill like a small mountain. At the crest of that hill, silhouetted against the fading orange sunlight, a tree larger than anything Amy had ever seen before stretched into the sky. The tree, by itself, seemed to be the size of a mountain, blocking out a chunk of the sky. Its branches reached so high into the heavens that she couldn't see them all, shrouded as they were in the clouds.

It was the Tree of Worlds. They'd found it!

But there was a problem. In the valley's bowl, stretching out before them and for miles to either side, was a vast dragon city.

Orange-gold fires sputtered from torches and braziers along streets, sending up streams of black guttering smoke. Stone rooftops and hard, dry mud walls reflected the fiery light of the setting sun. Herd animals of every kind milled about in nervous agitation in rock-walled pens.

Everywhere, absolutely everywhere, there were dragons. They glided through the air on leathery wings. They walked through the ashy dirt streets, swinging their spiky tails. Their scales shone like rainbows of glittering jewels from open windows and courtyards or even lounging in the sun on the roofs of buildings.

"But . . . but . . . this isn't supposed to be here!" Amy sputtered. "It's not on the map!" She rummaged in her bag and drew out the map to double check.

"There's no way to get around it," Flax said, staring out at the enormous dragon city.

Amy flattened the map against her legs. "This isn't supposed to be here! I'm sure of it!" she said, her voice high-pitched with stress. "The tree is marked, but there's not supposed to be any giant dragon city next to it!"

"What difference does it make?" Flax asked, shooting a look at her. "That map could be hundreds of years old for all we know."

Amy kept looking between her map and the city, hoping the city would realize its mistake and vanish immediately.

"Amy, it doesn't matter if it's on the map or not. It's out there. Are you going to try telling those dragons they aren't supposed to be here because your map says so?"

Amy scowled. She was about ready to do just that. "I was just saying—"

"There's no way to get around it," he said, shading his eyes and squinting into the distance. "It looks like there are still more buildings circling around that hill in both directions. I bet the hill is actually in the middle of the city, like the royal palace is in the middle of Tuleris."

Rolled the map back up and stuffed it into her bag. "But I have to get to the tree."

"I don't think there's any way through this, Amy. You can't fly. And those dragons will smell us for sure if we try to sneak through on foot."

"It's the only way! I have to go through that city."

Flax opened his mouth to argue some more.

Amy cut him off. "You don't have to come with me."

His mouth snapped shut. He blinked at her. "What?"

# CHAPTER EIGHTEEN

Flax stared at Amy with his mouth hanging open. "What do you mean? Of course I'm coming with you. Don't you want me to?"

Amy looked down at the hazy, smoky dragon city, then beyond to the hill where the Tree of Worlds blocked out the red sky. The delicious smell of roasting meat wafted up from the fire pits below, and her stomach rumbled.

She swallowed and looked at Flax. "You're running low on magic. You wouldn't be able to protect yourself from the dragons. I can't ask you to go down there with me. Maybe you can fly over and meet me on the other side."

Flax growled in frustration. "You want to go through that alone? Are you trying to get yourself killed?"

"Well, it might not be as bad as it looks."

"How can it not be as bad as it looks? Don't you see all the dragons? Don't you remember how easily the last ones could smell you?"

"I know, but we have to find some food, and the dragons have food down there. So maybe that's the best place to get some."

Flax stared at her blankly. "That is the worst idea I've ever heard in my life."

"I don't know what else to do! We can't just stay here! I have to get to the Tree of Worlds. So when it gets dark, I'll sneak through on foot and you can fly over and meet me on the other side."

Flax ran his hands over his face. "Not a chance. I can't let you go through there on your own. I may not be at full power, but it's better than . . ." He stopped talking and looked away with a sigh.

Amy frowned. She knew he'd been about to say, "Better than nothing." That was all the good her magic was to them. Even Flax saw her magical ability as nothing. She blinked tears out of her eyes.

She kept arguing with him for a while, but Flax refused to budge. She couldn't convince him to fly over the city on his own. As the last of the daylight faded to black in the western sky, they set off down the hill together, right into the dragon city.

As darkness descended around them, the flaming torches, blazing fire pits, and red-hot burning braziers seemed to grow brighter. The valley glowed orange like the inside of a volcano as Amy and Flax made their way down the steep, rocky hill. The surrounding air warmed with every step they took, filling with the dense smells of smoke, hot rocks, spices, and cooking meat.

Amy's stomach twisted with hunger as she wiped sweat from her brow.

"Ugh, I hope we get through this fast. It smells awful," Flax grumbled.

"It doesn't smell that bad. It's kind of making me hungrier. And I'm more worried about the dragons anyway," Amy said.

"Yeah, that too." He shrugged, wrinkling his nose.

From a distance, the dragon city had looked almost like a place where humans would live. The torches looked like something you might see in a fantasy movie. The mud and stone buildings looked like the kind people might have lived in long ago. The dirt roads seemed wide enough for horses and wagons to travel on and ran in straight or slightly curved lines between the houses and shops.

As they drew closer, Amy realized she had been mistaken. First, she noticed that the flames in the torches, though bright, looked much too small. They guttered and flared, but seemed always to stay close to the burning heads.

Next, she noticed that what she'd taken to be bushes

outside some of the fancier houses were actually fruit trees. Lemons, limes, and oranges flashed in the firelight between the dark-green leaves, but they only grew halfway up the height of the door frames.

When they got closer, she noticed chunks of meat turning on a spit over a bed of glowing coals by one building. When she looked more closely, she was shocked to realize that they were whole animals. Cows, sheep, and pigs were sizzling and dripping over the fire.

The city was enormous, not only in how far they'd have to go to get through it, but also in scale. Everything in the city was huge, like they'd traveled to a city of giants. The doors were taller than a normal human house. The roads were wider than the length of several full-sized school buses. The torches lining the roads were more like tall, burning trees.

Amy and Flax made it to the first house in time to scurry behind an enormous clay pot before a dull green dragon walked past. Amy couldn't help but think that they were like two mice huddling in a dark corner, hoping not to get smacked with a broom.

"So, here we are," Flax whispered in her ear. "Now what?"

Amy rested her hand on the smooth side of the clay pot—the thing was twice as tall as she was—and leaned out so she could peek around the corner.

"I guess we just keep going like we were before. We

have to stay hidden and only move when no dragons are looking. It'll be kind of like hide-and-seek."

"Okay. If you say so," Flax said, looking over her shoulder with wide, terrified eyes.

For the next several hours they skittered from hiding place to hiding place, building to building. Even though the sun had set, there were still dragons walking up and down the roads and flying overhead. Amy and Flax scurried behind boxes, pots, and display stands, hid behind the bushy fruit trees, and huddled in shadows. The going was slow, and they had to stop frequently to wait while enormous dragons walked by, scraping their sharp claws in the dirt and swinging their spiky tails.

At every turn, the smell of smoky roasted meat grew thicker. At many of the buildings, the dragons were preparing vast amounts of food like they were preparing for a feast.

Meat wasn't the only thing on the menu, though. There were bowls of huge plump berries and brown nuts, fresh vegetables, and even soups and pies, along with the roasting meat that filled the air with delicious smells. The warm, fragrant scents wrapped around them like a cozy blanket. Amy wasn't sure whether she was more sleepy or hungry, but all she could think about was stuffing herself with food and crawling into bed.

"I don't know how much longer I can take this," she said after they'd darted behind a tree planted against one of the dragon's homes. "I'm so hungry. The smell of that meat is driving me crazy!"

Flax looked around, and then up. "Aha! How about this?"

He reached up and plucked a few bright-yellow lemons. He stuffed one into his mouth, took a big juicy bite, rind and all, and handed another to Amy.

"But . . . that's a lemon," Amy said, uncertainly.

"They're good! Humans eat lemons, don't they?" he asked around a mouthful of juicy fruit.

Amy turned the lemon in her hands with a small grimace. She was so hungry by now she was willing to try anything. "All right. If you say so."

She sank her teeth through the rind and into the cool gushing center. Sour juice flooded her mouth, along with a few hard lemon seeds.

"Oh! Ugh!" Her mouth puckered. Her jaw clenched and ached. She spat out the lemon and continued spitting in a hopeless attempt to get rid of the horrible sour flavor.

"Well, if you don't like it, you don't like it. You don't have to make such a big deal about it." Flax rolled his eyes and stuffed the rest of his lemon into his mouth.

Amy wiped her tongue on her sleeve and gagged. "It's awful! How can you eat that?"

"What's wrong with lemons? They're tasty and

refreshing after a hot day." He shrugged and bit into another lemon, wiping dribbling juice from his jaw.

Amy watched him, wrinkling up her nose. Her stomach clenched and grumbled with hunger.

Flax stuffed a few extra lemons in his sack. "Maybe we'll find something you can eat. We just have to keep going."

"Yeah, okay."

How long had it been since she had an actual meal? Her legs wobbled and her head spun. If she didn't eat something soon, would she faint from hunger? Would she be able to keep going at all?

They continued sneaking between the giant-sized dragon houses. The farther they went, the nicer and fancier the buildings got. The stones were smoother. The walls were more even tones of white, brown, or black. The road went from flat dusty dirt to being paved with dark stones. And the houses got even bigger. Instead of simple buildings with a few rooms, they were now huge, sprawling structures with courtyards, fountains, and colorful mosaics on the walls.

The road they were traveling along grew more confusing as they went, too. It curved around the mansions and sometimes forked between them to rejoin itself on the other side. Other times, the road seemed to disappear altogether, splitting off into small branches that led into open courtyards.

When this happened, they usually had to backtrack to find the road again. It was time-consuming and frustrating, not to mention dangerous since it forced them to travel the same stretch of road multiple times.

When Amy poked her head out from behind a stack of clay jugs and realized they were inside another one of the dragon courtyards, she growled to herself and stomped her foot. "Really? Again? Can't these giant lizards make a straight road?"

Flax poked his head around to look. "Yeah, that smaller path over there is the one we should have taken. I guess we'll have to go back again. Um . . . I think if we follow the wall back to the corner, we can get on the right road from there." He turned to lead the way.

"Wait a minute," Amy said, grabbing his arm.

He looked back.

"Look over there. Through that open door. There's another door open on the other side of the room. Do you see?"

She pointed to the far side of the courtyard, where an open doorway led into a dim room. On the far wall of that room, a stream of pale early morning light fell through another open doorway. It looked like it led right out to the road.

"Amy," Flax whispered. "I'm not sure it's a good idea to go through a dragon's house. See the bowls and skewers and things? That's got to be a kitchen. If you go in there, you're just begging the dragons to cook you for dinner!"

"But there's all sorts of stuff to hide behind. See?" She pointed at the doorway. "See the sacks and pots and boxes? Loads of hiding places. And if it's a kitchen, maybe I can find something to eat in there."

Flax raked his hand through his hair and looked between the doorway and back the way they'd come a few times. "Well, we do need to find you some food," he said reluctantly.

A gust of wind stirred up the dust in the courtyard. Amy and Flax huddled behind the pots in case the wind came from approaching dragon wings.

The gust blew through the open doors, and a wave of scent crashed over them. Delicious, smoky, meaty smells swirled around Amy, and her stomach clenched.

She tightened her fists and nodded. "Let's do it."

A smooth stone wall bordered the courtyard between their hiding place and the dragon's kitchen, clear of any plants or barrels or boxes or anything else they could hide behind. A single stone pillar stood at the halfway point, supporting an upper balcony. The pillar cast a flickering shadow in the torchlight that danced on the wall like a dark ghost.

They waited a few heart-pounding moments to be sure the courtyard was quiet and empty of dragons, then they made a dash for it.

The door was much farther away than it had looked.

Amy pumped her legs, trying to put on greater speed. Flax launched himself into the air, wings humming, and tugged on Amy's arm to help her along. Their hiding place kept getting farther away, and the door kept getting closer. It seemed like one of those horrible dreams where you run as fast as you can for safety but never actually get there.

When they made it to the stone pillar, they paused in its shadow to catch their breath.

As they crouched there, panting and gasping, something shook the ground with a thump.

Amy grabbed Flax's arm in terror. Both of them froze in place.

A huge green dragon stomped closer. It paused and sniffed the air. Then it turned its head to eye the open doorway to the kitchen. "Hmm. Something smells good," it rumbled, and continued on its way, swinging its long, barbed tail after it as it walked.

When it turned the corner, Flax let out a breath and leaned back against the pillar. "That was close."

Amy gulped and took in a shaky breath. "Yeah. We should hurry and get out of here."

Flax met her eyes, nodded in agreement, and they made another dash for it.

They scurried along the stone wall, praying that no

more dragons would choose that moment to enter the courtyard and find them.

In a few heartbeats, they bolted through the kitchen door and into the gap between a sack resting on the floor and the inner wall of the kitchen.

Amy peeked out to examine their surroundings.

The room resembled a fairy kitchen, only with a lot fewer things that could catch fire. The shelves were stacked with jars of spices and tied bundles of herbs hung from the walls. There were tables and pots and pans and bowls and glass jars everywhere, but the countertops towered so high above her she couldn't quite see everything.

The far door stood open to their left. To their right, an enormous pit of glowing coals shimmered with red-orange heat. Turning on a long spit over the coals, several whole fat pigs dripped and sizzled as they cooked low to the ground.

This was what Amy had smelled from outside. The sizzling pigs smelled like bacon and glazed ham. The delicious aroma made her think of Christmas dinner and summer barbecues. Her mouth watered.

"Okay," Flax said, still glancing around for dragons. "If we head straight for the door from here, I think we can make it. It looks like there's a bunch of potatoes in that basket. You can eat those, right?"

Amy licked her lips, still looking at the pigs. "I want to get some of that pork."

Flax wrinkled his nose in disgust, then collected himself and sighed. "But that's all the way on the other side of the room."

"I'm not going to eat raw potatoes! Eww! It'll be fine. The dragons aren't here. Just wait for me by the door, okay?"

Flax clenched his fists and looked around the huge, empty room again with his jaw tight. He nodded at Amy. "All right. Just be quick," he said, then he hurried for the exit.

Amy crept toward the glowing coals and roasting pigs, making her way under shelves of cookware and behind enormous clay jars big enough to swim in.

As she drew close to the sizzling meat, she opened her bag and brought out her little stone knife. If she could cut a few strips of pork off to eat, she knew she'd feel so much better.

The shelves she was hidden under came to an end several paces before she reached the pigs. She hesitated, looking all around and listening for any sound of approaching dragons.

She could see Flax crouching by the back door, ready to bolt out of there as soon as she was done. He waved a hand for her to hurry.

She swallowed, took a deep breath, tightened her

fists in an effort to stop them from shaking so much, and walked out of the shadows toward the blistering heat of the coals.

The pigs were turning slowly over the heat, low enough for her to touch them if she wanted to. A thick metal bar skewered through them. Their legs were tied together to keep them from dangling into the fire.

Clutching her little knife tight in her fist, she stabbed the blade into the glistening skin of the nearest pig.

The skin was tough. Her knife barely made a dent in it. She tried again, but her knife slipped sideways and hot pig grease smeared over her fingers.

"Ow!" She shook her hand and hissed in pain, then licked the hot grease off.

It tasted amazing.

"Amy!" Flax's voice came from somewhere in the shadows by the door.

"I'm trying," she said, probably not loud enough for him to hear. She didn't want to get some dragon's attention by shouting, after all.

Flax waved to her and said something else, but she couldn't make it out over the distance.

She shook her head and held up a finger for him to be patient for a minute. Then she wielded her knife one more time and stabbed it into the crease where the pig's hind leg met its body. The skin there was thin, and it sliced open like tissue paper, sending out a gush of grease that sputtered in the fire.

Laughing with delight, she sliced off a chunk of tender meat with crispy golden skin and stuffed it in her mouth. The grease burned her lips and tongue, but she didn't care. It tasted every bit as delicious as it smelled—better than any pork she'd ever eaten before in her life.

Flax waved his arms from his hiding place by the door. He looked nervous.

"Okay, just a minute. I'm coming," she mumbled.

Before leaving, she decided to slice off one more piece of pork to take with her. Who knew when they would find edible food again?

When she raised her blade to slice into the pig's haunch again, a dark shadow suddenly fell over her.

She paused, knife raised, and lifted her eyes to see the shape of a huge dragon's head looming overhead. Its bright, glittering eyes were focused right on her.

Amy screamed. She tried to bolt back to the cabinets, but the dragon was faster than she was. Its claws swooped down and caught her up in a scaly, impenetrable cage.

"Ha!" the dragon snarled. "I caught it!"

# CHAPTER NINETEEN

Hot, scaly claws lifted Amy into the air. She tried to scream, but the claws squeezed her middle so tight she couldn't get any air. She tried to punch and bite her way to freedom, but the dragon's hard, scaly armor was too tough to do any actual damage.

"Eww. It's wiggling," the dragon rumbled in its deep, growly voice. It shifted its claws as it carried her, grasping her around the head and chest, and Amy could finally suck in a quick breath.

Through the gaps in the claws, she caught glimpses of the dragon's kitchen. She strained her eyes, hoping to spot Flax flying out to rescue her.

Her heart sank when she remembered that Flax was running low on magic. He might not have enough to save her from a dragon now. It would surely take a powerful spell to get the dragon to release her and let them both escape.

"What are you mumbling about in there?" growled another dragon from the doorway.

The claws holding Amy kept shifting and poking her as the dragon moved her around, apparently trying not to harm her. Amy tumbled in its grasp, her hair falling over her face. She could barely tell what was happening around her.

"I thought I smelled a fairy in here," the dragon holding her said. "But this isn't a fairy. Look what I caught trying to eat our pigs!"

The claws opened up and Amy felt herself falling. She grasped one of the dragon's sharp talons to save herself, but it shook her loose and she dropped onto a pile of prickly yellow straw.

She swept her hair out of her face and found that she was sitting inside something like an enormous birdcage. It was the right size for her, considering she was the same size compared to the dragons as a pigeon was to her.

Two dragons, one bright red and the other muddy brown, stood over the cage, staring at her with shining, predatory eyes.

She scrambled back on her hands and feet until her back pressed into the bars of the cage farthest from the dragons.

The brownish dragon bent closer and cocked its head. "It looks like a fairy to me."

"But the smell! Smell that!" The red dragon, the one that had caught her, sniffed the air in her direction, sending out little puffs of smoke.

The brown dragon sniffed cautiously while the red dragon chuckled and licked its chops.

"What is that thing?" the brown dragon asked, sniffing harder.

"It's a human!" the red dragon said, still chuckling.

"There's never been a human on Dragon Island. Never! Not a live one anyway."

"Well, this one is smaller than I would expect. Maybe something's wrong with it." The red dragon reached into the cage and started picking at Amy's things. Amy tried squirming away, but it was useless. The dragon was too big and strong. It took her bag, yanked off her cloak, and started tugging at her dress. "Just imagine when I bring an actual human dish to the summer festival. I'm bound to win the treasure this year!"

The brown dragon snorted. "If you want to keep it fresh, you ought to leave those things on it."

"Eh? Why would I do that?"

"If it is a human—which I'm not even sure it is—it's going to be a pathetic, weak creature that can't survive in the air on its own. That's why they cover themselves with that stuff."

The red dragon made an annoyed, disbelieving face. "Can't survive in the air? I've never heard such ridiculous nonsense!"

"Suit yourself. Just don't say I never warned you." The brown dragon snorted a puff of black smoke at the red one and stalked out of the kitchen.

The red dragon watched the other go, then looked at Amy uncertainly for a moment. It shook its head, grumbling, and fastened the latch on the cage, leaving her with her clothes.

The dragon walked to the other side of the room and flipped through a set of thin stone tablets on the wall. Finding the one it was looking for, it pulled the tablet down and examined rows of marks carved into it that looked like simple runes.

"Hmm, smaller than it should be. Not deformed or diseased, though. Could it be a juvenile? O-ho! I'm sure that would make the meat extra tender!"

With her whole body shaking and her heart hammering behind her ribs, Amy rolled to her belly and pushed herself up onto her knees.

The straw lining the floor of the cage smelled stale. Dry lumps of animal dung dotted the floor here and there, but she was too frightened to care about that.

She grabbed a bar and quietly pulled herself up to her feet. The metal bars that held her in looked slender when compared to the cage, but they were actually as thick as the rungs on a ladder. There was no way she could bend or break them to escape.

She leaned against the wall, gripping the bar with one hand and wiping her tears away with the other. After a few moments, her hand tingled and itched. She let go of the metal and curled up in the smelly, crinkling hay, hugging her knees against her chest.

The red dragon bustled about the kitchen gathering cooking supplies, pots, a pile of onions and garlic, hot peppers, and spices. Now and then its shining golden eyes flashed to Amy, and it grinned and chuckled in a self-satisfied manner, sending puffs of black smoke from its nostrils.

Flax was still nowhere to be seen. Amy cast her eyes about the kitchen, wondering if he was hiding somewhere nearby. Part of her hoped he was crouching out of sight with a brilliant plan to break her free. Another part hoped he'd flown far away from this horrible place.

"This will do nicely," the dragon said in its deep, growly voice. It turned back to the cage, holding bright red and green fruits in one of its claws. In the other, it held a metal key. With a deft flick, it unlocked a door near the top of the cage and dropped the fruits in. They thumped and bounced on the floor when they landed.

Amy yelped and scrambled back.

"Mmm. Eat up, little human," the dragon said, locking the door again. "That will add a little sweetness to the flavor, I think." It ran its long tongue over its dripping chops and padded out the back door, leaving Amy locked in her cage, alone in the empty kitchen.

She cowered against the wall, gasping and gulping with fear. Then her hunger got the better of her and she crawled toward the fruits. They were mangoes. She picked one up and ripped away the tough outer rind to get at the flesh.

As she ate, she examined her cage more closely. The dragons seemed to think she was some sort of animal. If they thought she wasn't any smarter than a cow or a chicken, maybe they left an easy way for her to escape.

She kicked the bottom of the bars where they met the floor of the cage, but they didn't budge. They were welded in place. No luck there.

The door was near the top of the cage. Even though the dragon had used a key, she thought she might unlatch it from inside if she could get up there. She climbed the bars to reach the latch, but halfway there her hands itched and burned so badly from the metal she couldn't stand it.

She dropped back into the straw and blew on the red burning skin of her palms.

"Amy!"

Amy's head snapped up at the sound of Flax's strained voice.

He hovered outside the cage with his wings blurring behind him. His face was pale with fear.

"Flax! You're here!"

"Of course I am! I'm here to get you out!"

"They locked the door." She pointed at the metal door above her. "I thought I could unlock it, but the—"

"I got it!" Flax zoomed up to examine the lock. "Looks simple enough. A little tweaking and I can get that open. Stupid dragons. They think they're the only ones with brains. I'll just reach my hand in and—"

"Wait!" Amy cried.

"What?" Flax paused with his hand an inch from the lock.

"It's iron," she said.

"You're sure?"

She held up her palms, showing him the red painful blisters forming.

Flax winced. "Ouch. I forgot. Dragons do use iron sometimes."

"Maybe you could touch it just long enough to open the door?"

He shook his head. "Iron hurts fairies a lot more than . . . well, I'd have to use a lot of magic to heal myself. And I'd rather not have to do that."

"But Flax—"

"Hold on," he said, brightening. "I'll find something to wrap my hands in! That way I won't have to touch it at all." He zipped away before she could say anything else.

Amy took a deep breath and shook her head. It wouldn't do to sit there arguing when the dragons could come back at any moment. If his plan worked and he didn't have to get burned at all, that would be better anyway.

Flax zoomed around the kitchen, hovering over the various surfaces as he looked for something to wrap his hands in. With how small he was compared to the dragon's kitchen, he looked like the tiny fairies in movies and TV shows. Amy almost laughed, watching him.

He found a few pieces of cloth, but they were much too large. The dried herbs were too brittle. Finally, he settled on a stack of broad, fresh banana leaves, pulled out his knife, and started cutting one into long strips.

Amy paced back and forth along the bars of her cage as she watched him. Every few seconds, she glanced back at the open doors.

"Come on. Hurry!" she whispered.

"Almost done," he muttered as he started wrapping one hand in a green strip of banana leaf.

Amy glanced at the door again and froze.

A huge, brown, toothy snout poked through the door of the kitchen. It sniffed and poked in a little farther, revealing a scaly head and shining eyes.

Flax and Amy looked at each other in terror.

The head moved in, followed by the brown dragon's long, sinuous neck. Its gold, gleaming eyes narrowed. It sniffed again, and the eyes snapped to focus on Flax where he sat on the table.

"Fairy!" the dragon roared, baring its teeth and lunging into the room. It opened its mouth and a stream of fire spewed through the air, blasting the stone tabletop right where Flax had been sitting a moment before, consuming the stack of banana leaves.

Flax had jumped out of the way just in time, zooming across the room in a wobbly, panicked arc.

The dragon followed him, scrambling across the floor, spouting gouts of flame, catching some of the wooden objects in the kitchen on fire, tumbling over stacks of clay bowls, breaking pottery, and knocking supplies off tables.

In his panic, Flax darted behind a clump of hanging herbs. When the dragon spewed fire again, the flames engulfed them, leaving nothing but a clump of brittle ash and a black scorch mark on the wall.

Flax screamed.

Amy watched, horrified, as his smoking body fell down the wall and landed behind the counter.

"Where did it go? Where did it go?" The dragon rumbled frantically, scrabbling things off the countertop with its front claws. It sort of reminded Amy of how her grandmother reacted when she spotted a spider in her house.

"What's going on . . . WHAT ARE YOU DOING?" another dragon's voice roared from the doorway. The red dragon stood there with its wings half unfurled, glaring at the brown one.

The brown dragon stopped and looked around guiltily at the smoking, messy disaster in the kitchen. Items were scattered all over the floor. Food was spilled everywhere. Several things were actively on fire, and several others were burned completely to ash.

"Th–there was a fairy!"

The red dragon snorted derisively.

"It's true! There was a fairy! It was cutting up the banana leaves. But I think I got it!"

The red dragon looked at the stack of banana leaves on the counter. It had been a stack of banana leaves, anyway. Now it was a pile of shriveled gray ash.

The red dragon narrowed its eyes and pointed at Amy. "That . . . is a human. Not a fairy. Can't you smell straight?"

"Rutile, listen, I—"

"Enough! Just help me clean this mess and carve up the pigs before they overcook. We'll need to pull out some more banana leaves, too. Ugh!" The red dragon gave a final snort and shook its head.

The brown dragon stretched its neck to peer behind

the cabinet one last time before grumbling under its breath and helping to clean up the mess.

The two dragons tidied up the kitchen, patting out a few flickering fires with their bare claws.

Then they spent the next few hours carving the roast pigs. They cut and wrapped heavy chunks of pork in fresh banana leaves, stacking them in big leather satchels for transport to the summer festival.

Amy continued pacing along the wall of the cage, craning her neck to see the counter where Flax had fallen. The sound of his scream still echoed in her ears. No matter how hard she tried, she couldn't see him.

"How do you suppose it got to the island?" the brown dragon asked. It glanced at Amy as it carved a chunk of pork with one sharp claw.

The red dragon shrugged dismissively. "Some legends say that humans have magical abilities. Others say they steal magic from fairies when they can. If that one has some magic, it could have gotten here on its own." The red dragon shuffled its wings and stuffed some more pork in its satchel. "Or maybe another dragon broke the law and went to the human world to hunt one. In that case, the human could have escaped someone else's kitchen. It doesn't matter to me how it got here. What matters is that I caught it, so I get to cook it." The red dragon grinned, showing all its pointy teeth as it sliced a claw into the roasted pork.

A queasy feeling writhed in Amy's gut.

Still, she kept looking for Flax. Maybe she would catch a glimpse of him if she kept watching. Maybe he'd wave at her to let her know he was okay. She hoped the dragon hadn't burned him too badly. She hoped he was still alive.

"Are you going to start a stew tonight, then?" the brown dragon asked. "The longer it simmers, the more tender the meat, you know."

"I've been thinking about that," the red dragon said in a low, pleased rumble. "I'm feeding it mangoes to sweeten the meat. If I keep it fresh right until the moment of the contest, then I can wait to sear its tender rump extra rare on a hot stone."

Amy shrank back and reflexively grabbed her rump as though she could protect it.

"Sounds delicious," the brown dragon said, licking its chops.

"The king will go mad when he tastes it. I'm sure to win the prize this year."

Both dragons turned to stare at her with their unnerving cat-like eyes.

Amy whimpered and scrambled to the back of the cage, keeping out of sight as they chuckled and continued carving the pigs. Their sharp claws made wet, slicing sounds as they worked, cutting into the flesh.

Amy couldn't help but imagine those claws cutting into her before they served her up for dinner.

AMY COULDN'T REMEMBER FALLING asleep, but she woke, curled up in a prickly pile of old smelly straw, when the cage rattled, shook, and lifted off the counter.

She yelped and jumped to her knees, blinking bleary eyes. Stalks of straw clung to her hair and dress.

The red dragon was carrying her through the kitchen and out the back door into the cool morning light.

Amy scrambled to the cage wall, careful to avoid touching the iron bars, and looked down at the floor by the counter where Flax had fallen the previous day. She could still see the dark patch on the wall where the dragon had blasted it with fire, but there was no sign of her friend.

The cage swung around, then dropped with a sudden jerk when it landed on some sort of walled platform. Looking around, Amy saw that a lot of other supplies surrounded her cage, mostly from the kitchen. Pots and jars, baskets and bags, folded fabric, jewels, metal tools, and thin stone tablets. The platform looked a lot like an enormous wagon or cart, but with handles protruding from both sides.

She barely had time to wonder what was happening when the two dragons, wearing harnesses tied to the cart, grabbed the handles in their front claws and beat their wings, lifting themselves and all their supplies into the air.

"Oh, no! Where's Flax?" She ran to the back of the cage and stretched to her tiptoes, trying to see over the wall of the platform, but it was no use.

The brown dragon shot her a narrow, suspicious look with its shining eyes and she cowered back meekly. She wanted to scream insults at them and demand to be released, but she knew it wouldn't do any good. It might even give them an excuse to cook her right now instead of later.

The wind grew colder as they rose into the sky, shifting from a hot summer day to a brisk winter morning in a matter of minutes. Amy curled into a ball and shivered as she tried to keep warm.

She couldn't stop thinking about Flax and that horrible scream before he fell in the dragon's kitchen. Was he still there, lying burned and motionless on the floor among dusty old bits of food like a dead spider? Was there something she could have done to save him? She should have listened to him. She never should have gone for that pork in the first place.

She sobbed into her knees and let her tears soak into her dress. There was nothing she could do for him now.

Some time later, they landed, and the dragons started unpacking the cart.

The first thing Amy noticed was the noise. Growls, rumbles, roars, flapping of leather wings in the air, whooshing of wind, even the flamethrower sound of dragon fire filled the air. The second thing she noticed was the smell. Mixed in with the sulfur smell of dragon fire was the thick aroma of charred meat and hot spices. Wherever they had gone, there were other dragons here. Lots of other dragons!

Her captors placed the cage on a flat stone near a cooking pit in the shade of a tent, and she saw that this place differed greatly from anywhere else she had seen on Dragon Island. So far, the land had been sparse, with charred ashy soil and hardly any trees or bushes. In comparison, this place was overgrown with trees and flowers and bushes of all kinds.

She turned to look all around and noticed a dark stone castle on a neighboring hill. Black and purple flags fluttered in the breeze from the spires. Dragons of every color imaginable swarmed around it with their scales shining in the sunlight. In the opposite direction, towering like a mountain over them and much closer than she had seen it yet, the Tree of Worlds blocked out half the sky.

"Now," the brown dragon growled, shuffling its wings, "how do you plan to cook the human, Rutile?

You'd better start preparing soon before one of these rock-lickers gets a whiff of it and steals it from you."

The red dragon swiveled its head around and looked at Amy. A slow grin showed rows of sharp, glistening teeth.

# CHAPTER TWENTY

"Be patient, Pyrochlore. This dish needs to be fresh and hot when I present it to the king," the red dragon hissed between its teeth.

"But the human will only attract attention from every dragon that comes to our stall!"

"If you think one of these dragons is foolish enough to steal from me, why don't you guard the little beast?"

The brown dragon, Pyrochlore, narrowed its eyes and puffed out a short blast of black smoke, but didn't press the issue. It grumbled under its breath as it stalked past Amy's cage. "Smoke and flames, Rutile! If you want to let someone steal the thing, that's none of my business."

After they'd unpacked the cart and had everything set up, the two dragons got to work selling their pork. Other dragons lined up at their stall, jaws dripping, to exchange bits of gold or small jewels for a serving of meat. Amy's captors added spices and sauces to the packets of pork on request, making the whole place smell like delicious, spicy curry.

Amy wasn't thinking about eating anymore. She sat trembling at the edge of the cage, trying not to touch the iron bars. Some irrational part of her brain thought that maybe if she didn't draw attention to herself, the dragons would forget all about her and she'd manage to escape somehow.

Even though she curled up as small as she could and held as still as possible, every dragon that visited the food stall sniffed the air and exclaimed when they saw her, "Is that really a human? Where did you find it? Can I buy it from you? I'll pay anything for it!"

At first, Rutile seemed happy with the attention. The red dragon preened and waved off the attention with false modesty. "Oh, that? A little something I've been saving for a special occasion. I thought the king would like something more exotic this year."

As time went on, more and more dragons came to gawk at Amy, and none of them wanted to buy anything at all. After a few dozen of these visitors, Rutile snapped. "That's it! I can't deal with these gawkers anymore. Hide that human somewhere! Cover it up!"

Pyrochlore gave a smug smile and snorted, then grabbed the cage and carried it to the back of the stall.

Amy lost her balance and fell to her hands and knees as the cage rocked.

The brown dragon lifted a big sheet of leather next to some bags and baskets and stuffed the cage underneath, hiding her from prying eyes. It draped the leather over her cage, leaving a small gap to the outside through which a shaft of daylight beamed down into her prison.

Amy wondered if the brown dragon left the gap on purpose so she'd have some fresh air, the way her dad would punch holes in the lids of glass jars so she wouldn't suffocate the bugs she caught.

Thinking about her dad made tears stream down her cheeks again. What was her father doing now? Was he worried about her? Would she ever see him again? She wished she could go home.

When her tears finally stopped falling, she wiped her cheeks with her hands and went to the side of the cage, trying to get close to the sunlight streaming through the gap in the leather.

Her burned fingers brushed against the cold iron bars.

"Agh! Ouch!" She sucked in a hiss of pain and shook her hand. Then she held it in the light and looked at the blisters on her palm where she'd grabbed the bars when trying to escape.

She might not react to iron as badly as a full fairy would, but it still hurt. She could heal the burns herself, though. Since her body already knew how to repair itself, she wouldn't have to use a spell. It would use up some of her magic, and it wouldn't do much good since the dragons were getting ready to cook her anyway, but it wasn't like her magic could do anything else helpful right now.

She pulled on the chain of her talisman, drawing the creamy white stone out from under her dress, and let her magic flow through it. She focused her power back into her own body, willing it to heal the damage where the iron had touched her skin.

Her magic went to work right away, doing what her skin was already trying to do, soothing the pain, removing damaged skin, generating new cells at an astonishing rate. Her palms and fingers tingled and a warm sensation, like sun-baked honey, oozed over her skin. After a few moments, her hands were as good as new. She flexed her fingers and rubbed her palms against her dress, feeling more hopeful without the pain distracting her.

"Since I can still use my magic, I might as well try to break out of here while I can," she mused. "Maybe if I try to change the color of the bars, they'll explode and I can just walk away."

She paced around the perimeter of her cage, squinting in the dim light and trying to find a weakness she could use her magic on. Finally, she decided to go with her first idea. Maybe it would actually work and the cage would explode like the water orb and the rose bush had. If not, the dragons might pull back the leather to find a green cage with red flowers. Maybe that'd freak them out enough to let her go.

She held her talisman in her hands, took a deep breath, and focused on the iron bars, trying to sense them the way Cypress had instructed her.

After a few moments, her brow furrowed, and she frowned. This wasn't right. It was the most bizarre thing she'd ever felt with her magic.

In her mind, the metal of the cage felt like bitter, numbing, cold blackness. It felt the way her mouth had felt after getting a cavity filled at the dentist.

She shivered and bit her lip in concentration, trying harder to feel the structure of the bars, to understand how they worked and what held them together so she could make changes. It was like there was a void there, a bottomless pit that her sense of magic couldn't touch.

She gave up trying to sense anything. Maybe cold, tingling emptiness was what iron felt like. If she failed to sense it properly, that would only help her magic to fail worse, which was what she was going for, anyway. Maybe the bars would melt into goo or crumble into dust.

There were also horrible and dangerous things that might happen. The cage might catch fire or turn into a puddle of deadly poison, but she didn't want to think about that.

She imagined the metal changing from dark, rusty gray to a bright, bubblegum pink color.

In response, the empty void hummed and vibrated in her mind. It was a strange sensation, but not painful.

She gathered her magic and let it surge into the surrounding cage, willing the spell to work.

Nothing happened.

Nothing happened at all.

Amy staggered a little at the sudden drop in her power. She'd put a lot of effort into that spell. Surely something should have happened! Even when her spells went horribly wrong, something always happened. She'd half expected the cage to shrink down to the size of a mouse and crush her, or to grow ten-foot-long spikes and skewer her like a marshmallow, or to explode like a bomb and tear her to pieces. She'd taken a huge risk using magic on it, knowing that the spell would go wrong somehow, but how could her magic do nothing at all?

She decided to try a different spell. This time, she decided to put a spell on two of the bars, softening the metal so she could bend them apart and crawl through.

She focused on the bars, shivering at the empty, tingling sensation, and pushed her magic into the spell. This time, the spell was much smaller and took less magic, but still, nothing happened. The cold iron bars stood rigid and completely unchanged, like they were laughing at her attempts.

"Oh, come on!" Amy griped. "Do something!" She grabbed a handful of straw and threw it at the bars out of frustration.

She tried a spell to turn the cage into sugar candy. She tried another to warp the metal, so the door would move down to the ground. She tried another to make the metal vanish into nothing.

With every spell, the iron bars soaked up her magic like rain falling on gravel.

She growled, pulled at her hair, and kicked one of the bars with her shoe. Then she crumpled to the floor, feeling weak from using so much of her magic and defeated by the stupid bars of her stupid cage.

This was it for her. If she never got out of there, no one would ever know what had happened to her and Flax. Why did she ever have to drag Flax into this mess? He could have stayed home, but as far as she knew, he was still lying burned under the dragon's kitchen counter like some sort of gross bug.

Some other fairy should have come to Dragon Island to get a piece of wood from the Tree of Worlds—some fairy that could do magic better than Amy. Any other fairy in Titania would have been a better choice than her, the half-human girl who couldn't do spells. She was so useless she couldn't even get herself out of a simple cage!

Flax had tried to tell her how dangerous going to Dragon Island would be. He'd been terrified of the idea, but he'd gone with her anyway because he was a good friend. He was a better friend than Amy was by far. He never would have pressured her into doing something so dangerous.

Amy sobbed into her knees as she prayed fervently that Flax wasn't too badly injured, that he'd survived the dragon fire somehow, that he found his way safely back home.

She almost didn't hear a whispered voice calling her name.

"Amy! Psst! Amy! Are you hurt?"

She threw her hands back, jerked her head up, and skittered away from the sound in shock.

From the darkness behind one of the huge clay jars, a shuffling, scraping noise came. Then a dirty, bedraggled, tired-looking Flax limped into the dim light. He was dragging a huge metal key.

Amy gasped when she saw him and scrambled over to the bars nearest to him.

"Flax! You're . . . alive!" At the last moment, she stopped herself from saying all right. He clearly wasn't all right. His left arm was blistered with burns. His clothes were charred. Some of his hair had been singed off and nothing remained of his wings but pathetic black stubs.

"I used a spell to protect myself from the fire. It didn't work very well." He grimaced and brushed some ash from his clothes. "And now I barely have magic left at all."

"Oh, Flax," she sobbed. Tears started streaming down her cheeks again. "I'm so sorry. Does it hurt a lot? I should have listened to you!"

"Don't worry about that now," he said, clenching his teeth and limping up to the side of the cage. "You need to get out of there before the dragons come back. I found the key to the cage in one of their baskets." He lifted the key to show her. The handle was wrapped in a long, slender leaf to keep his hand from touching the metal.

"The lock is all the way up there." She pointed up at the hinged metal door of her cage. "But the whole cage is made of iron."

"So how can we get the key up there and open the cage?" he asked.

"Could you do a spell?"

Flax started shaking his head.

"I mean, I know you're out of magic, but what if you start a spell and I feed some of my magic into it? Like your idea for pulling pranks in the palace garden?"

Flax sighed and leaned the key against the side of the

cage. It was so big it could have been a sword. "It would work if the key wasn't made of iron. Fairy magic doesn't work on iron. Not at all."

"It doesn't?" That explained why none of her spells had done anything to the cage.

"Also, a spell that would get the key into the keyhole, turn it, and open the door would take a lot more control than I have. I couldn't do it even if it was made of wood."

The sound of dragon feet thumping into the ground silenced them for a moment. The dragon came close. They could hear its breath and rumbling voice outside the drape covering the cage. Then it stalked away again.

Amy swallowed, panting in shallow breaths, and turned to look at Flax. The whites of his eyes shone in the dim light.

"I'll do it," she whispered.

"I told you magic won't work."

She shook her head. "Not with magic, with my hands. There isn't time to think of another way."

She reached through the bars and grabbed the key. Then, taking a deep breath to steady herself, she started climbing the iron bars of her cage.

Flax choked out a soft cry when her hand closed around the dark metal, but it didn't immediately burn through her skin the way it would him.

At first, her hands sort of tingled and itched. She

climbed up a couple of rungs, passing the heavy key from one hand to another on the outside of the cage.

By the time she got to the third rung, the bars felt like they were coated in tiny fire ants, stinging and burning. She rubbed her palms against her dress in between steps and hauled the key up another level, then another.

"You're almost there, Amy!" Flax said, pacing on the ground below her.

Her hands were really burning now. Every time she touched the metal bars, it felt like running a bad sunburn under hot water. She gasped and whimpered, but she forced herself to hold on and push herself up another metal rung.

She made it to the bottom of the door, set at an angle into the peaked roof of the cage. Climbing up to the lock would mean dangling from under the tilted roof.

She rubbed her burning palm on her dress and grabbed the bottom rung of the cage door. It wobbled when she put her weight on it and her hand slipped. She tried to catch herself with her feet, but her balance was off. Her feet slipped from the iron rung, and she dropped.

"Amy!" Flax croaked in a dry voice.

The giant key saved her.

Gripped tightly in her fist, the iron key jammed

between two bars and jerked her to a stop, dangling in place halfway up the wall of the cage.

Her body slammed into the lower bars, making a huge rattling clanging noise. She scrambled to get her grip back, swinging her legs wildly to find the rungs again.

"What was that?" a dragon rumbled from outside. Amy recognized the sound of Rutile's voice.

"Probably just the human trying to escape," Pyrochlore said in a dismissive tone, like it was nothing to be concerned about.

Amy finally got her feet under her and pushed herself back to a standing position. Her wrist throbbed where the iron bars had pinched it. Both her palms burned. She could feel blisters forming on her skin, and the cage door was still over her head.

"Better go check on it. We can't risk it getting loose," Rutile growled quietly.

Amy and Flax stared at each other for a breathless moment, then Amy started climbing again, faster this time, desperate to get to the door before the dragons caught them. Her palms blazed with every grip she took, but she ignored the pain. She bit down on her lip in concentration as she climbed up to the level of the door.

"Pshaw! Let it try. There's no way to get out of that cage!" Pyrochlore said. "It was made to contain fairies."

Getting the key to go into the keyhole turned out to

be a lot harder than she expected. The blisters in her fingers popped, leaving her hands slippery and even more painful than before. The heavy key wobbled as she tried blindly to align it with the lock on the opposite side of the door. She pressed her body against the iron bars, gripping the key in both hands as she tried jamming it into the keyhole, but it didn't want to go in.

"Amy!" Flax said, "I think it's upside down!"

She groaned and rotated the key so the teeth faced the other way.

"Just go get it. It's about time to prepare it anyway," Rutile said in a growl.

"Hurry!" Flax cried.

"I'm trying!"

The key went in. Amy squeezed the cold iron shaft, sending searing pain through her hands, and twisted it with all her might.

The key turned. The lock gave a very satisfying click.

Suddenly, the leather drape covering the cage lifted, flooding the area with blinding sunlight and cool air.

The brown dragon stood over them and examined the cage with suspicious green eyes.

## CHAPTER TWENTY-ONE

Amy froze in place, clinging to the key and not even noticing the pain in her hands anymore. Flax stood perfectly still on the ground.

The brown dragon lowered its head to look at her.

"It's climbing the wall of the cage," the dragon said with an amused growl. "Are humans smart enough to know how doors work?"

"Maybe," the red dragon answered. It was standing by the counter where the rest of the pork waited to be sold. A bed of coals glowed red on the ground nearby, ready to cook a fresh human delicacy. "The legends say they can even use tools. I've heard some birds are that smart. Maybe humans are too. Just bring it here."

The brown dragon hooked its claws into the bars of the cage to lift it.

At that moment, three things seemed to happen at

the same time. Flax jumped into the open, waving his arms wildly and shouting, "Hey, lizard breath!" The dragon snarled in alarm. And Amy pushed the cage door open.

"The fairy!" Pyrochlore bellowed, glaring at Flax. "It followed us here! I knew I saw one! Kill it!"

Amy jumped out of the cage and landed on the hard dusty ground with a pained groan. In an instant, Flax gripped her arm and pulled her to her feet.

"Come on! We have to run!" he yelled, just as the first blast of dragon fire scorched the air over their heads.

Amy screamed, and Flax yelled in terror. Together, they darted between jugs and boxes, racing to get away from the enraged dragon.

Behind them, Amy could still hear Pyrochlore snarling, "Get the fairy! Kill it!"

Fire spewed through the air with a rumbling roar. Flames engulfed the box to their left, singeing the hair on Amy's arm. The blast of heat in the air made the fresh blisters on her hands scream in pain.

They scrambled between stacks of clay pots and gaps in leather canopies while all around them dragons roared in surprise or rumbled in confused irritation. Heavy stomping claws shook the ground. Tails smacked into tent walls and knocked over boxes and jars as they scurried about looking for the source of the trouble.

Amy and Flax squeezed through a gap between two

crates, only to come face to face with a green-scaled dragon. Its nose twitched, and its amber eyes widened in surprise. “It’s true! There is a fairy here!” it said.

Amy and Flax turned and ran as another gout of fire whooshed by. It blasted the leather side of the tent, searing through the material like wet tissue. The flames dripped from the supporting ropes and seemed to pool on the ground, forming blazing puddles in the dirt.

Amy tugged on Flax’s arm, leading him around another corner and away from the fire.

“Stop it, you fools! You’ll burn my human!” Rutile bellowed in the distance, barely audible over all the chaos.

Everywhere they went, dragons were swarming all over the place, cursing and snarling, kicking up dust and debris, blowing gusts of wind with their wings. The calamity actually made it easier to hide.

There was so much commotion, so many bright gouts of flame, burning tents, scrabbling claws, flapping wings, whipping tails, pots and pans toppling over, clumps of grass and leaves swirling in the wind, and shining scales flashing that none of the dragons spotted the small human and fairy racing underfoot.

They kept on running, dodging the stomping claws, sharp talons, and swinging tail spikes. Amy’s chest ached and her throat grew raw with thirst, but she pushed herself to keep going. The sounds of snarling, crashing, and roaring fire faded behind them, but they continued running. It didn't matter where they were going. All that mattered was that they were getting away from the dragons and their horrible feast.

Flax stumbled and fell now and then. Amy helped him up every time and never let go of his arm, pulling him along with her even though it felt like the skin of her palms had been burned clean off.

How long they ran, Amy couldn't be sure. It felt like hours or even days. Eventually Flax stumbled again, and when she tried to pull him up, he collapsed to the ground with a quiet sob.

"I . . . I can't," he gasped as she tugged at his elbow.

Amy looked around wildly. What if the dragons were still after them? What if they were following their scent like giant scaly bloodhounds? But there were no signs of dragons nearby, and they couldn't keep running forever, especially since Flax was injured.

Now that she was looking at their surroundings, she noticed that they had ended up in a sort of park or garden. Large bushes and tall trees were growing around them. A shallow, bubbling brook flowed into a clear pond off to their right. Crimson and purple flowers flashed from the ground and bloomed from bushes all around. Weathered white marble glinted in gaps between the trees and jutted out from the ground like old stumps. Though worn from centuries of rain and wind, the crumbling marble still bore decorations carved here and there, hinting that this was where an ancient castle or palace had once stood.

Flax cradled his burned arm, gasping in pain.

Amy grimaced. She needed to heal him while they had a chance.

"Okay," she panted, still trying to catch her breath. "Let's at least find somewhere to hide."

She helped Flax stand, and he leaned against her while she helped him to a sheltered place behind one of the marble walls.

Flax crumpled to the ground as soon as they got there, gasping and shaking.

"I can't," Flax said, weakly. "I can't run anymore. I'm too weak. It hurts too much."

"It's okay. I think I can fix that," she said, pulling out her talisman.

Flax blinked at her in confusion as she gently laid her hand on his shoulder.

She concentrated, letting her magic flow into him, giving his body the energy to knit his flesh back together and regrow his wings.

When she finished healing him, she took a moment to heal her own blistered hands again, breathing a sigh of relief as the pain faded away and new skin grew over her raw wounds.

"You . . ." Flax blinked, flexing his new wings experimentally. "You can use your magic to heal. I can't believe I forgot that!"

She smiled wryly at him. "Yeah, I know. Healing doesn't take a real spell, so it's easy."

He chuckled, looking sort of embarrassed. "It isn't easy. It takes a lot of power. If I tried healing myself like that, even if my magic was all the way full, it would have taken almost everything I had. I should have remembered you could do that, though. I guess I was just used to thinking—"

"That I couldn't do any magic?" she finished for him.

He shrugged and gave an apologetic smile. "Sorry."

A screeching sound made them both look up. A group of dragons was soaring overhead, their green and orange wings translucent in the sunlight. They screeched calls to one another and started sweeping back and forth over the trees.

Amy and Flax scrambled under a nearby bush to get out of view as the dragons passed by.

"They're looking for me," Amy whispered.

Flax shook his head. "They might like to catch you for dinner, but they hate fairies. Those dragons are furious. I'm pretty sure they're after me."

They cowered together under the bush for a few more minutes, watching the sky through the gaps between the branches of the trees. Now and then swarming dragons flew low overhead, sending gusts of wind into the woods and shaking the leaves on the outstretched branches.

"We need to keep moving," Flax whispered after a while. "They'll find us if we stay here."

Amy nodded in response, but neither of them made a move to leave their hiding place. Finally, when there seemed to be a lull in the dragon activity, they crept out from the shelter of the bush. Hand in hand, they hurried deeper into the woods, away from the smoke and chaos of the dragon's summer festival.

The ground sloped upward in front of them, making walking difficult. Amy panted for breath as she trudged ahead, taking swigs of water now and then.

Why were adventures always uphill or in deep dark caves or through icy cold water? If she had to run for her life, it would be nice if it was over a gentle downhill slope, preferably with soft moss to land on if she tripped.

At the crest of the hill, the Tree of Worlds stretched so far into the sky they couldn't even see its topmost branches, shrouded in mist and cloud. The farther up the hill they went, the less Amy worried about the dragons chasing them and the more she was interested in their surroundings.

They passed by jagged chunks of marble scattered around the forest floor, crumbling walls, shattered white columns, and old dusty fountains. In some places where the rain had washed away the earth, beautifully paved roads shone through in brilliant white and onyx black. It seemed like the woods surrounding the tree used to be an ancient city.

"You know, I'm starting to think we might actually make it," Amy said, shielding her eyes as she stared at the tree towering into the sky. "The Tree of Worlds is right there. We'll probably get there before sunset."

"It's still possible," Flax said. "Tamarind said the dragons guard the tree, but maybe all the dragons are at the festival."

Amy bit her lip and furrowed her brow. She didn't want to have to face any more dragons. Not now. Not ever.

Flax saw her face and shrugged, flashing a crooked grin. "But even if there are dragons guarding the tree, I'm sure they won't be expecting two kids to try sneaking in."

Amy stopped walking.

Flax stopped, too, and turned to look at her. "Hey, don't worry. I'm sure we can figure something out."

Amy pointed ahead of them, up the hill, and Flax turned to see.

The trees were thinning the farther up the hill they went. In the gaps between their trunks, a smooth stone wall peeked through.

Unlike all the white marble ruins and rubble scattered everywhere, this wall looked whole and clean, without a crack in it. It looked new.

Flax jumped into the air and flew ahead, keeping low to the ground. Amy jogged after him, staying in the shadows of the overhanging branches in case any dragons flew by.

"What is this?" Flax asked, zooming back and forth along the white stone wall.

"It's a . . . wall," Amy said.

She reached out her hand to feel the surface. The cool white stone felt very smooth. Not as smooth as glass, but there was no way she'd find handholds to climb up, even if she had the strength. After everything they'd been through that day, she wasn't sure she even had the energy to climb a ladder, let alone a wall.

She looked in both directions. The wall seemed to continue on to the right and left without end.

Flax grunted impatiently. "I know it's a wall. Obviously it's a wall. But what's it doing here? The tree is on the other side!"

"Can you fly over it?"

He looked up and around and snorted. "It goes higher than the trees. If I tried to fly over it, those dragons would see me. And I'd rather not get my wings fried off again."

Amy winced at the thought. "Yeah. Okay. I guess

we'll just have to follow it and see if there's a way around. Maybe there's a gate or something."

They turned left and walked along the wall for a while, following its gradual curve around the crest of the hill. Birds sang in the garden-like forest around them. Now and then, a breeze blew drafts of air from over the wall, sending a sweet floral scent from the other side.

Stumbling with exhaustion and hunger, they finally found what they were looking for. A massive, sparkling gate, as tall as a three-story building and as wide as a two-car garage. It was so beautiful that Amy stopped to stare open-mouthed. Colorful jewels, sparkling in the soft forest light, shone from the black bars and golden designs. Strange angular runes ran up the outer posts, and intricate pictures, too small to understand from a distance, decorated the upper arches.

In the gaps between the bars, Amy could see a wide cobblestone path bordered with flowering bushes and trees, leading ahead toward the center of the garden and the Tree of Worlds.

"We're almost there," Amy whispered, squeezing Flax's hand in excitement. Hope flared in her chest. It was all worth it. They'd come through greater danger than they'd ever been in before. They'd made it to Dragon Island on their own, escaped from the dragons who wanted to kill and eat them, and finally found the

Tree of Worlds. It was right there. All they had to do was go through the gate.

She took an eager step forward, pulling Flax with her.

His grip tightened suddenly, and he jerked her back.

"Huh?"

"Shh!" He put his hand over her mouth and pulled her back behind a crumbling marble wall, crouching low. "Look over there," he whispered, pointing to the left of the golden gate.

On either side of the gate, bright green bushes with violet flowers grew close to the stone wall. Similar bushes dotted the forest all around, so Amy hadn't paid any attention to them. The clump of shrubs to the left of the gate was larger than most, and there was something else strange about it. Twin streams of pale smoke drifted into the air from the shade of its leaves.

Amy stared harder.

Something moved in the bushes. As she watched, a dragon's head, emerald-green with purple fringe, rose out of the leaves, blinking its amber cat-like eyes.

Amy's heart thumped. Her mouth went dry. Her eyes widened. She couldn't look away. The dragon was stunningly beautiful, like a jeweled statue coming to life.

Flax said nothing, but his hand tightened and his breath shuddered. Amy could tell he was panicking. She wanted to say something to help, but she couldn't get her voice to work either.

The dragon turned its head to the downhill slope of the forest with a fierce rumble in its throat, baring its white pointed teeth.

"We have to get past that dragon," Amy finally whispered in barely more than a panicked breath. "Maybe we can wait for it to go to sleep or . . ."

Flax swallowed. His eyes were open wide and his hand trembled in hers. "Amy, I think that dragon is royalty."

"What? What do you mean?"

"Dragons have kings and queens, just like fairies do. My teacher said that the better a dragon eats, the brighter and more colorful its scales get. Only royal dragons can eat enough to develop purple colors."

"Okay. So this dragon has pretty colors. So what?" She shrugged. "We've seen a lot of dragons in all kinds of colors here."

He shook his head. "Eating so much also gives them a lot of strength and sharper senses. Plus, it looks like this dragon is here on purpose to guard the gate. I don't think we'll be able to sneak past it."

Amy peeked over the ragged top of the wall. The dragon was casting its shining eyes about the forest as though looking for the source of a strange sound or smell. "Maybe there's a way we could distract it.

Maybe we could get it to go away from the gate for a while."

"I don't have enough magic left to spell the whiskers off a kitten, Amy, let alone stop a dragon," Flax said, holding his hands out helplessly. Then he perked up a little. "What about the spear?"

Amy crouched down next to him, wrinkling her brow. "The dragons took my bag from me when they put me in the cage."

He pulled the bag off his shoulder and unbuttoned it. "Yeah, and they stuck it in the basket I was hiding in. I have it here." He pulled out the ornate black and gold spear, shuddering when he touched it, and handed it over to Amy. "The magic in that thing feels . . . fierce."

She tapped the ruby, and the spear snapped to its full length. She could feel the magic crackle sharply, like jolts of static electricity against her palms. It thrummed with wild, intense magic.

"If this spear is enchanted, it might be the perfect weapon to slay a dragon," Flax said.

"Slay?" Amy's eyes shifted from the golden designs on the spear to Flax's face. "You mean, you think we should kill the dragon to get past it?"

He shrugged. "It would try to kill us the second it saw us. Killing it would be self-defense."

Amy bit her lip and looked down at the spear again. The swirling dragon designs and sparkling jewels sort of matched the ones decorating the gate. Why would dragons make a spear to kill other dragons?

Then again, humans used to make swords for war. Maybe the dragons used spears like this when they fought one another. As if breathing fire that could melt rock and having scales like armor and talons like knives wasn't enough.

She shook her head. "I don't know, Flax . . . I'm not sure I could kill a dragon, even if I had a magic spear."

"Who goes there?" the dragon bellowed in its snarling voice.

Flax and Amy ducked lower behind the marble wall and went still.

"Speak now or feel the wrath of my flame!" the dragon roared.

Amy squeaked out a terrified whimper, but neither of them dared show themselves. The moment the dragon saw them, it would all be over.

# CHAPTER TWENTY-TWO

The dragon slithered out of the bushes, revealing vibrant purple wings and shining green flanks. The ground shook as it stamped a claw into the earth. It looked around, baring its gleaming teeth and thrashing its tail.

"Speak now or I strike!" the dragon roared.

"Oh, don't be such a wet fog, Opal," said another dragon's voice. This one came from the woods downhill of where Amy and Flax cowered. "We just came to see the Tree of Worlds."

There was a muffled snuffing noise as another dragon stifled a chuckle.

The guard dragon, Opal, snorted in displeasure. "Garnet? What are you doing here? Aren't you supposed to be in the fortress with your father? And it's Princess Opal to you, and don't forget it."

Two new dragons strode out of the trees into the clearing, approaching the dragon at the gate. One of them was a glistening black, so dark it looked like polished black diamonds. The other was a greenish-brown that faded to pink along its crest and wings.

"Oh, how could I possibly forget that?" the brown and pink dragon sneered. "All those years saying you were my friend, then your father takes the throne and suddenly you're Princess Opal and I'm nothing but a lowly apprentice warrior."

So, Flax was right. The dragon was royalty. And she was a princess just like Amy.

Princess Opal hissed, lowering her head and flaring her wings. "It's not like that! I'm still the same dragon I always was. But—"

"Then why don't you let us through to see the tree?" Garnet asked, cocking her head in mock innocence. "My old friend, Opal, would have let us through. My friend would even come with us and have some fun for once." Garnet's tone was still bitter and mocking but laced with an undercurrent of pain.

"You know I can't do that," Princess Opal growled. "Only royalty with the proper authority may visit the Tree of Worlds. It's my obligation as heir to the throne to guard the gate during the summer festival. It's tradition. And I mean to take it seriously, even if you don't."

She narrowed her shining eyes at both Garnet and the black dragon.

"I bet she doesn't even know," the black dragon muttered. A smile crept up his muzzle.

Garnet wrinkled her snout in a wicked grin. "I think you're right. No one's told her yet."

"What are you talking about?" Opal demanded. Her purple crest flared and her eyes darted between the other two.

Garnet laughed. "I heard a rumor that the new queen of fairies is coming with an army to settle some imaginary dispute with us. She's probably using it as an excuse to attack and take control of the tree." She snorted. "I hope she does. A real battle might liven things up around here. Not that you'd be able to join in, since you'd be busy fulfilling your duty by sitting up here all on your own." Garnet tapped a claw at her chin thoughtfully. "But the fairy queen is royalty, after all. She may even have the gate key. Are you saying you'd let a disgusting fairy go through the gate but not us?"

Amy's heart jumped. Her breath caught in her throat and her gut twisted. Did that dragon just say her mother was coming?

Of course, her mother was coming. When the guards failed to bring Amy home that first night, her mother wouldn't have let it go. And when Amy and Flax disappeared for days with no word, she wouldn't have rested until she found out where they went. She probably had spells that could tell her exactly where Amy was at any moment. Amy should have known that her mother would go anywhere and do anything to protect her.

She still hadn't expected her mother to come to Dragon Island! In the open! With an army! What if they started a whole new war over this?

At Garnet's words, Opal jerked her head back and choked out a black cloud of smoke. Apparently, this was surprising news to her, too.

"You really didn't know about that, did you?" Garnet sneered.

The black dragon chortled. "She's stuck out here, away from everyone and missing all the important stuff."

"Don't you think our princess ought to be informed of these things?" Garnet asked in a tone of pretend concern.

Princess Opal raised the spiny frill along her back and lifted her head, puffing out another cloud of smoke. "Guarding the tree is where the princess is supposed to be during the summer festival. The Tree of Worlds is important to all the realms. I will do it faithfully."

Amy reluctantly realized that she sort of liked this dragon princess. Sure, she was fierce. If Amy came out of her hiding place, the dragon would probably kill her the moment she saw her. But Princess Opal had a sense of honor and duty, and Amy admired that.

"Oh, come on, Opal!" Garnet whined, throwing her head back dramatically. "I thought you'd be more understanding. I even promised Onyx you'd let us through!"

Opal narrowed her shining eyes, turned in a slow circle like a cat, and rested her haunches in front of the gate with her wings unfurled to block the way. "Then you shouldn't have made that promise."

Garnet sighed and shot Opal a resentful look, then turned to walk back down the hill. "Come on, Onyx. Let's go."

The black dragon swiveled its head around to look at Garnet, then turned to glare at Opal. "We're going to leave? Just like that?" He lifted his lips in a snarl. "I came all the way from Firefall Cliffs to see the tree. She can't stop us!"

Garnet stopped and turned back, nose wrinkled in annoyance. "She's being a slimy worm about it, but I can't make her let us through."

Onyx snorted a laugh, sending out a wisp of orange flame that curled up his muzzle.

"What's she going to do, kill us if we try to get past her?" he asked. He shook his head and swaggered a few steps closer to the gate.

Opal's eyes narrowed at him in a wary glare.

Garnet's mouth dropped open in alarm.

Onyx coiled himself back on his haunches with a smug grin and leaped at the gate, flapping his midnight black wings to sail over Opal.

"Onyx! No!" Garnet yelped, pivoting around and thrashing her tail in alarm.

A vicious snarl ripped from between Opal's bared teeth. In a blindingly fast move, she sprang into the air and unfurled her purple wings, launching herself at the black dragon.

Onyx's wings stalled mid-flap, like he wasn't sure whether to drop lower or try to gain more altitude to avoid the charging dragon.

In his split second of indecision, Opal pulled her lips back from her teeth and brought her rear claws forward to strike him with all four sets of razor-sharp talons.

She crashed into him midair.

It was hard to see what happened next. Opal's wings flapped forward, engulfing Onyx as they spun together in the air. Amy saw that Opal's teeth closed around the black dragon's neck, piercing through scales and squeezing into muscle.

Onyx squealed a single yelp of pain and shock before his voice choked into silence. They twisted and writhed in the air for a moment, and then they fell.

Opal's claws pinned his leathery black wings to his sides. Onyx lashed his tail wildly, but it was useless. He couldn't escape her hold.

Opal tilted her wings to guide their fall, so that Onyx was on the bottom with her weight above him when they landed.

They crashed down. A deep boom shook the earth, mingled with a horrible, crunching snap, like a tree breaking in half.

"Onyx!" Garnet screamed, leaping across the clearing.

Onyx lay in a crumpled heap on the ground with Opal's jaws still fastened on his throat. His eyes were wide and wild. A trickle of blood dripped from his open mouth.

"You killed him! How could you?"

Opal gave the black dragon one final shake with her jaws before releasing him and stepping back. Onyx sucked in a breath and bellowed in agony.

"Onyx! Are you all right?" Garnet said, prodding him with her nose as he rolled over and staggered to his feet. One of his wings wasn't folding properly. It hung limply from his shoulder and dragged on the ground.

"What did you do to him?" Garnet demanded, snarling at Opal.

Opal snarled back and answered slowly, voice seething, "I did my job, just like I said I would. Now leave!"

Garnet stared at Opal for a moment, resentment turning to bitter hatred in her eyes. Then she nudged

Onyx with her nose, and the two of them slowly made their way back down the hill.

"I . . . I thought you said she was your friend," Onyx said, coughing. Wet blood glistened on his neck where Opal had bitten him.

"No," Garnet growled. "I was wrong. She isn't my friend. I don't think she ever was." She cast one more nasty look back at Opal before bracing herself against Onyx to help him walk back through the forest, away from the gate.

Princess Opal watched them go with her head high, her jaw tight, and her wings spread to block the gate. When the other two dragons vanished down the hill, her hard expression cracked into a slow, heartbroken grimace.

She paced in a tight circle and lowered herself to the ground in front of the gate. A small patch of dragon blood dampened the grass next to her. She didn't seem to notice it. Her wings folded over her sides, her tail wrapped around her legs, then she let out a long, rumbling sigh.

"Now it's right in front of the gate," Flax murmured in Amy's ear. "There's no way we can sneak past it."

Amy glanced down and the long dragon spear was glinting in her hand. Somehow, the thought of using it to kill Princess Opal seemed wrong, but what other choices did they have?

"Hold on, Flax. I have an idea. If you make a spell to turn us invisible, could I feed magic into it so we can sneak past the dragon?"

He pursed his lips in thought. "Yeah, I could do that. But I can't stop the dragon from smelling or hearing us. The spell I know would only make us invisible."

The wind shifted, rustling through the branches overhead and cooling the skin on Amy's face and neck.

The dragon snorted and looked up. Her head swiveled around and her eyes darted over the bushes and rubble in their general direction.

Amy and Flax crouched behind their chunk of marble wall, exchanging a worried glance.

"Do you think she saw us?" Amy whispered.

"Smelled us is more likely," Flax said quietly. "Maybe heard us. I don't know." He gulped.

Amy bit her lip anxiously. Then on a whim, she grabbed a chunk of marble from the forest floor and hurled it as far as she could into the trees, across the clearing from her and Flax.

The piece of marble crashed through the bushes and tumbled through the dry leaves scattered over the ground.

Opal's head snapped away to face the noise.

Amy did it again, picking up a rock and aiming for the same spot.

The dragon's eyes narrowed at the noise. She scrambled to her feet, shaking out her purple wings and spreading her claws, preparing to fight again.

This time, Flax picked up a rock and hurled it a little to the side of where Amy had been aiming, making it look like some creature was moving around in the underbrush.

It worked. Opal stepped forward, uncoiling her tail as she stalked toward the source of the noise, leaving the gate clear.

"I'll start the spell now. Feed your magic into it and I'll hide us," Flax whispered urgently. "This might work if we go before the dragon gets back."

Amy nodded and laid her hand on his shoulder. She felt his spell flicker to life, weak and faint, and gathered her own magic to feed steadily into it.

Instantly, they were invisible. She looked down but could no longer see her own body, only the forest floor below them. Flax seemed to vanish next to her, but she could still feel his warm shoulder under her hand.

"Let's go," Amy whispered.

"Right," Flax's voice said out of seemingly empty air.

Walking when you can't see your feet is a lot harder than it sounds. If they'd been in the royal palace of Tuleris, with its smooth, even marble floors and nothing to trip over, Amy would have been happy to run straight ahead. She'd know there wouldn't be anything to trip over.

Here, in woods scattered with treacherous roots, chunks of marble hidden under piles of leaves, thorny bushes, and mounds of soft dirt, running was out of the question when their legs and feet were invisible.

They walked forward, taking extra care so their feet didn't crunch in dry leaves, rustle bushes, or topple stones that might make noise.

From their hiding place behind the broken marble wall, the dragon's gate had looked alarmingly close. Now that they were trying to make it there before Opal returned from investigating the mysterious noises, it seemed impossibly far away.

Amy squeezed Flax's arm as she urged him to walk faster, feeding magic into his spell. They weaved between bushes and over rough stones, avoiding dry sticks or anything else that might crunch under their feet and give away their location.

Opal eyed the forest where the stones had crashed and sniffed a few times. She rumbled, pushing her snout through the bushes and sniffing some more before she swiveled her neck around to look back at the gate. Her yellow eyes landed right on the place where Amy and Flax were walking.

Amy bit her tongue to keep from screaming. Her grip on Flax's arm tightened a little more.

They were almost there! The jeweled bars of the gate stretched into the sky right in front of them. The bars were wide enough that she and Flax could probably squeeze through them if they tried. A few more steps and they'd be there.

Her foot landed on a jagged root jutting out of the ground. Her shoe slipped on the smooth surface, making her lose balance. Her arms jerked, trying to keep her from falling, and she felt the fabric of Flax's tunic slip through her fingers.

She blinked, and suddenly Flax was standing, perfectly visible, next to her. His eyes met hers for a moment, then they both looked at the dragon.

Opal had turned to face them, glaring dangerously and puffing smoke from her nostrils. "What is this?" she rumbled, baring her teeth. "Fairies?"

"Amy! Run!" Flax screamed.

In an instant, he was in the air, flying in a low arc across the clearing.

Opal's snout followed him as she sucked in a lungful of air and took aim, preparing to torch him to a crisp.

He darted around her head, guiding her away from Amy.

"Fly away, Flax! Get out of here! You don't have enough magic to fight her!"

The dragon focused on Flax with rage burning in her eyes. She opened her jaws and let loose a gout of blue-white flames.

# CHAPTER TWENTY-THREE

The world slowed down.

The dragon's flared wings billowed like graceful seaweed in a slight current. The plume of white-hot fire arced through the air, at the pace of dandelion fluff drifting on the breeze. Flax's eyes widened little by little, reflecting the blazing firelight as he watched his doom close in. Amy could see the realization in his eyes. He knew that, without his magic, there was nothing he could do to save himself from the dragon this time.

Everything blurred and faded as Flax and the dragon's fire snapped into focus. Nothing in the world mattered but saving her friend.

Without stopping to think, Amy grasped her talisman in one hand and concentrated on the empty air between Flax and the stream of dragon fire. She pictured an invisible, impenetrable barrier shielding him from the flames. Then, not giving a moment's thought to whether or not the spell would work, she threw her magic into the air, willing it to do what she wanted.

Half an instant later, the blue-white flames crashed into a sphere-shaped shield of air, streaming out in all directions, and dripping to the ground like melted glass. Dancing motes of magic flew off the magic shield at the impact, like sparklers on the Fourth of July, but the spell held firm.

"Gah!" Flax yelped, throwing his arms up over his face and flinching back. Then, realizing that the fire hadn't touched him, he looked up, blinking in confusion.

Amy didn't wait to see what the dragon would do next. Clutching the dragon spear in her fist, she sprinted across the clearing, pushing herself forward with little bursts of magic, and skidded to a halt in front of Flax, facing the green and purple dragon.

All around them, branches of nearby trees crackled in flame. Smoldering ash littered the ground. Pools of dragon fire glowed and flickered here and there, sending out waves of blistering heat that sent the air swirling upward. Amy could hear Flax's panting breath behind her and the occasional buzz of his wings. He was safe. He wasn't hurt. That was all that mattered.

The dragon paced closer, eyeing the burning destruction in the clearing, then turning its fierce gaze on Amy with teeth bared and tail lashing. A deep rumble, like low thunder, came from the dragon's chest.

"A–Amy?" Flax's trembling voice came from behind her.

"You dare . . . YOU DARE come into our forest and approach the sacred tree? Filthy fairies! I'll DESTROY you!" Opal roared. She sucked in a deep breath, preparing to sear them with another blast of fire.

"Flax! Run!" Amy cried, and she sprang forward to meet the dragon's attack.

Flax jumped into the trees and Amy darted to the side, drawing the dragon farther into the clearing. The great beast turned her huge scaly head and blasted fire at Amy this time.

Again, Amy was ready with her shield spell. She could feel her magic draining as it resisted the incredible heat of the dragon's fire. She was already weakened from healing herself and Flax and trying to get out of the iron cage, so she knew she wouldn't be able to keep this up forever. She had to think of another plan, something that would stop this dragon for good.

The blast of fire subsided and Amy let her shield drop, but she kept running, trying to stay out of the dragon's line of fire, and also trying to keep her attention away from the woods where Flax was hiding.

Opal scrambled after her, hissing and growling, smoke spewing from her nose and mouth.

Then Amy remembered the spear. It was still there in her hand, thrumming with magic. Maybe this was what she needed. Maybe this was what it was meant for. It was the tool a fairy would need to get past the ferocious dragon guarding the tree. Maybe it was the only weapon powerful enough to take down a royal dragon.

Flax was right, after all. This dragon didn't hesitate before trying to kill them as soon as she saw them. They had to defend themselves.

Amy stopped and spun around to face the charging dragon, holding the spear out in front of her and aiming the sharp point at the dragon's scaly chest.

The dragon sprang forward, claws reaching out to slash her.

This beast had attacked Flax, Amy reminded herself. Other dragons had burned him, nearly killed him, and had been ready to cook Amy as part of their horrific summer festival.

The dragon's jaws spread wide. A blazing white ball of fire formed in the back of her open mouth.

Amy planted her feet and drew back the spear. She focused on a point below the charging dragon's neck.

At the last second, Opal's eyes shifted from Amy to the spear in her hand.

Her wings snapped open. Her jaws snapped closed, choking on a mouthful of smoke and flame.

Amy launched the spear, pushing a surge of magic on the spell she'd prepared in her mind. The long, glinting cylinder flew ahead. Then, with a loud bang that hurt Amy's ears, it shot forward like a bolt of lightning.

The spear struck the dragon's chest, right where Amy had been focusing. It broke through the scales like they weren't even there and exploded from the other side, where it embedded itself in the stone wall.

Amy froze and stared. She couldn't believe what she'd done.

The dragon let out a high-pitched keen of agony. She stumbled and fell, choking out black, greasy smoke and coughing up dark, sticky blood.

Amy watched in numb shock as the dragon twitched and clawed at the wound on her chest. It felt like none of this was real. Or if it was, it was happening to someone else, far away.

"Amy!" Flax's cool fingers closed around hers.

She turned to look blankly at him.

"Come on. We can go through the gate now," he said, tugging her hand.

She gulped and nodded. Yes. They were in danger. They had to go.

She let Flax pull her along toward the gate, still

feeling like this was all some sort of confusing nightmare.

The dragon writhed and coughed on the ground, letting out gurgling cries. Her wings scraped dust and smoldering ash into the air. Her spiky tail slapped against trees and into crumbling ruins as she twisted in pain.

They were halfway to the gate when Amy hesitated and turned back.

Flax jerked to a halt and stared at her, confused. "Come on! Before any more dragons show up. We're almost there!" He tugged urgently at her arm.

Princess Opal was still coughing and twisting in the dirt, but her movements were growing weaker. With every passing moment, she struggled harder to take in choking breaths. Blood oozed from her gaping mouth and from the hole in her chest. Her panicked eyes stared, glassy and unfocused.

Amy shook her head and followed Flax a few more steps toward the gate. Then she stopped and turned back again. She couldn't stand it. Her heart ached at the sight of the suffering dragon. She couldn't leave her to die like that.

Flax stopped again when she did. "Amy? What is it?"

"Flax, I want you to go on without me. Go find somewhere to hide, okay?"

"What?"

She turned to him with a serious frown. "Find somewhere safe. If you can get to the tree, do it. I'll be there in a minute."

Flax opened and closed his mouth, then choked out, "Amy, what are you doing?"

Amy shook her head. She didn't want to think about what she was doing. She just had to do it.

Releasing Flax's hand, she ran back, away from the gate, to the place where the enormous, jewel-colored dragon writhed in agony on the ground. Dark ichor seeped from her mouth as she twisted. Blood dribbled from the small hole in her chest where the spear had pierced her scales.

As Amy approached, the dragon's writhing slowed until she was barely moving at all. Dust settled over her scales, making them look dull and lifeless. Her pulse throbbed and stuttered in her neck. Her eyes stared, unfocused, into the surrounding trees.

"I can't believe I'm about to do this," Amy muttered to herself. "This is stupid. The dragon will just kill me."

The dragon's eyes slowly slid closed and a faint, pitiful whine escaped her throat.

Amy took a deep breath and let it out slowly. Then she grasped her talisman in her hand, stepped forward, and laid her free hand gently on the dragon's hot, scaly forearm.

The first time Amy had used her magic on purpose

was when her father was severely ill. He'd been dying of pneumonia in the hospital, and the doctors didn't think he would make it.

Healing magic didn't take a lot of skill, but it did take a lot of power. When Amy had used her magic to save her father, she'd had to sleep for almost a whole day to recover afterwards.

That was when she was full of magic. Not after trying to spell her way out of an iron cage, healing her blistered hands twice, healing her friend from burns and regrowing his wings, powering an invisibility spell, putting up two dragon-proof force fields, and shooting a spear through a dragon's chest like a bullet.

She was tired. She could feel already that her magic was dwindling. Maybe she wouldn't die if she ran out of magic, like a true fairy would, but she would be exhausted. She'd never been this low on magic before. Now, here she was, getting ready to use her magic to heal a dragon, a creature so wildly different from her that it would probably be ten or a hundred times harder to heal than a fairy or a human.

She closed her eyes and reached out with her magic, sensing the life in the dragon, all the intricate things that worked together to keep it alive, its blood, its breath, its fire, its mind, its magic.

Behind her, she could hear Flax shouting warnings, begging her to stop. But she could feel the dragon now.

She could feel how much Opal was suffering. She could feel how scared and confused she was, how she could sense the life flowing out of her, how she was in complete despair.

Tears sprang into Amy's eyes.

"Amy! Come on! Leave it alone! It's not safe!" Flax yelled.

Amy looked over her shoulder. Flax was hovering low in the middle of the clearing, ignoring her command to hide himself, but also apparently too nervous to approach the dragon.

She shook her head, and a tear streaked down her cheek. "I can't do that, Flax. I have to help." With that, she poured the rest of her magic into the dragon, willing her to heal.

The dragon's body knew what to do. It was already trying to heal, and Amy's magic gave it the power it needed to stop the bleeding, drain the fluid from the lungs, repair damaged flesh, mend broken bones, and regrow broken and missing scales.

Though he trembled with fear, Flax came closer to stand by Amy's side and laid a supporting hand on her arm.

Part of her was irritated with him for not listening to her when she told him to hide, but another part, a bigger part, was happy to have him with her.

As they watched, the wound in the dragon's chest

stopped bleeding. The damaged flesh knit back together. Bright new scales grew, replacing the broken ones. The dragon's eyes blinked and came into focus. A moment later, Princess Opal coughed and took a shuddering breath.

Amy's hand fell from the dragon's hot foreleg as a profound weariness washed over her. The trees seemed to spin around her head. Her legs felt like they were made of overcooked spaghetti. She staggered and stumbled back.

Flax caught her elbow and gently lowered her to the ground.

"All right. You did it. Now we need to run. You need to get up, Amy. I'm not strong enough to carry you now. We have to get out of here!" His voice was ragged with fear.

The world wobbled back into place in time for Amy to see Opal lift her head and stagger to her feet.

Amy tried to stand, but her legs felt all tingly and weird. They didn't want to cooperate.

The dragon turned a fierce amber stare on her, bared long, glistening white teeth, and lunged.

## CHAPTER TWENTY-FOUR

The dragon's teeth gleamed. Claws like spears slashed through the air. Smoke blasted in twin streams from her shining green nose.

Amy dropped to the ground, squeezing her eyes shut. After her last spell, she didn't have the energy to even try running.

Flax yanked on her arm, struggling to get her to move, but it was too late.

The dragon's teeth snapped together.

Amy clenched her jaw tightly and tensed her muscles, waiting to feel teeth and claws sinking into her skin.

But nothing happened.

She could feel wind whipping dust and leaves around her body, but that was all.

Hardly daring to breathe, Amy cracked one eye open and tilted her head back.

The massive dragon loomed over them. She spread her wings in a threatening stance. Her shining amber eyes bore right into Amy's, full of intensity and anger.

"Who . . . are . . . you?" the dragon said slowly, carefully enunciating each word. She lowered her nose and sniffed the air over them. "This one is a fairy. My nose tells me that much. But you're no human, no matter how delicious you smell. No human could perform magic like that."

With legs and arms as weak as pudding, Amy tried to scramble back away from the fierce glare of the dragon. Rocks and sticks poked into her palms and knees, and she could barely get herself to move. After spending so much magic healing the dragon, her head was spinning and stars flickered over her vision.

The dragon stalked forward one more step, keeping her eyes locked on Amy and Flax. She spread her purple wings and fanned them once, blowing up whorls of dust and leaves. "Answer me, creature. Who are you? What are you? How did you find that dragon treasure? Many lives have been lost for the sake of that key!"

"I . . . I'm just . . ." Amy panted, still trying to scoot away.

Flax tugged on her arm, trying to help her to her feet.

She blinked the stars out of her eyes and shook her head. "Wait. Did you say key?"

"Of course! The gate key is priceless dragon treasure, and it is rightfully ours!" She blasted smoke into the air. Blue flames flickered between her teeth. "Only royals with the authority to approach the Tree of Worlds are worthy to handle it."

"So it's not a spear at all . . ." Amy gasped.

Opal's lips pulled back in a snarl. She lowered her head to glare at Amy. "The treacherous fairies stole it from our treasury ages ago. We fought to get it back. Hundreds of dragons perished, and thousands of fairies. But the filthy beasts never returned the treasure. They even dared to deny they had it." Her eyes flashed to Flax with a look of pure hatred, then she turned back to Amy.

"Did you steal it from the fairies? Did they give it to you? WHO ARE YOU?" Princess Opal roared the last words so loudly it hurt Amy's ears, and even when she finished speaking, a rumbling growl continued deep in her throat.

Too scared to think of what else to do, Amy started babbling the truth. "I–I'm Amy. And you're right. I'm not a human. Not all the way. I'm half fairy. That's why I can do magic. My aunt gave me the spear—I mean key. She had it locked away. I'm really sorry I hurt you. It's just, we need to get to the Tree of Worlds, and you were attacking us."

Opal lowered her head and sniffed Amy's hair. "Hmm. So you are a halfling. Unusual. And you've brought proof that the fairies had our treasure all along. The gate key belongs here, with the dragons. Not with foolish, flighty tricksters!" She snorted in Flax's direction.

"But . . . we didn't know!" Flax said, looking first at the dragon and then at Amy. "I wasn't old enough to fight in the dragon war. What I learned was that the dragons made up an excuse to fight us because they hated us. Nobody even knew what kind of treasure they thought we stole."

"Well, Aunt Orchid did have the key, so they were kind of right," Amy said.

"Maybe she's the one who stole it," Flax suggested.

"She is pretty evil," Amy said with a frown.

Flax nodded thoughtfully. "And she was obsessed with destroying all the fairy doors. If she made it so we couldn't get to the Tree of Worlds, that would mean we couldn't make any more."

"What if she did it on purpose to start the war?" Amy said.

As they talked, Opal lowered her head so her shining eyes were looking right at Amy's face. "Am I to understand that you are related to Queen Orchid, halfling?"

Amy looked up at the sound of the dragon's voice. Then, with some effort, she stood on her weak, shaky legs.

For the past few months, Cypress had been drilling all sorts of royal fairy manners into her head. Everything from how to talk to guests at a party, to how and when to eat ceremonial meals, to how to greet visitors to the royal court.

She knew exactly how she was supposed to introduce herself as a visitor to another princess. She just never thought that the other princess might be a dragon.

Amy performed a slightly wobbly curtsy. Then she said, in as clear and confident a voice as she could manage, "I am Princess Amaryllis Porter, daughter of Queen Lily of Titania. It is an honor to meet you, Princess Opal. We have come to your domain on a quest to collect wood from the Tree of Worlds."

Opal arched her neck, keeping her snout pointed at Amy like a snake about to strike. "Now you claim to be fairy royalty? Why should I believe you? You came to our kingdom unannounced, with no court to attend to you and with no army to defend you! Even if you were a princess of Titania, why should I let you through the gate? The only reason I'm not flaming you both this instant is because you used your magic to heal me."

"Please," Flax said, bowing low to the dragon. "If I may speak, Your Highness."

Amy and Opal both turned to him—Amy in curiosity, and Opal with disgust clearly written on her face.

"As a fairy of Titania, I swear to you on my honor and by my magic, that this is Princess Amaryllis of Tuleris, daughter of Queen Lily, and heiress to the throne of Titania. She speaks the truth."

Opal wrinkled her snout doubtfully.

"She is royalty and approached the gate with the key. According to your traditions, doesn't that mean she has the right to enter?"

"Fairies and their tricks!" Opal snapped impatiently. "As if I would believe anything a fairy says!"

"Oh, come on!" Flax wailed, waving his arms in exasperation. "I swore by my magic and everything! Don't you know that means I can't tell a lie?"

While Flax argued with the dragon, Amy walked over to the wall where the key protruded from the smooth stone. She grasped it in her hand, feeling the powerful magic thrumming through the black material, golden decorations, and sparkling jewels.

She braced a foot on the wall and yanked hard on the key, jerking it side to side a little until it wiggled free of the stone. Then she turned to face the dragon.

Princess Opal flattened her wings to her sides and regarded Amy with narrowed, suspicious eyes.

Amy kneeled on the ground, bowed her head, and offered the key up with both hands. "I believe this treasure was stolen from your people. As princess of Titania, I am returning it with sincere apologies on behalf of my people. I don't know for sure how Orchid got it, but she isn't queen anymore, and my people don't want to be at war with yours. I think a lot of dragons and fairies suffered because of this."

The dragon stared down at her for a long, tense moment. Then she reached out with one claw and took the key from Amy's hands, examining it thoughtfully. In the dragon's claw, the glinting black and gold shaft was exactly the right size to be a key.

From the forest below, the sound of clear silver trumpets echoed in the still silence.

Opal turned her head toward the sound, then looked back at the key, then at Amy. "I suppose it's true you defeated me in single combat," she mused.

Amy winced. "Sorry about that."

The dragon chuckled and waved her free claw dismissively. "And you didn't have to heal me afterwards. You were well within your rights to let me die in shame."

"I never wanted to kill you!"

"So, it seems I owe you a favor," Opal said.

Amy exchanged an amazed look with Flax.

He laughed in disbelief. "Are you serious? You'll let us through?"

"I never said I'd let a common fairy through!" Opal snorted in disgust, baring her teeth at Flax.

"Oh, please!" Amy said. "He's my best friend, and he promised to help me!"

Another series of trumpet notes sounded through the trees, closer this time.

Opal shuffled her massive wings and lifted her eyes to the sky with a grumble. "Ugh. It goes against everything we hold sacred. But, if the male fairy is sworn by oath, then perhaps it's acceptable."

She turned to Flax again, speaking through clenched teeth. "Very well, if the princess wishes you to join her. But we must be quick. I hear the sounds of many dragons approaching the gate. It may be that others know you are here." She lifted her nose and sniffed at the breeze drifting up the hill. "From the sound and smell of it, there are fairies with them."

"The royal emissary!" Amy said. "They came here because of us!"

Opal nodded and started toward the gate. "That is very likely."

Amy gulped and twisted her fingers together as she trotted at Opal's side. "I'm going to be in so much trouble when they find me."

"They were going to find us eventually," Flax said. "Unless you were planning on never going home again."

She shot him an annoyed look. "Fine. But we at least

have to get to the Tree of Worlds first. I can handle being in trouble later."

Princess Opal glanced down at Amy and nodded with an amused smile, showing a few of her sharp white teeth. "I will delay them at the gate for as long as I can. And, Princess Amaryllis?"

Opal paused.

Amy stopped and looked up at her. "Yeah?"

"As Crown Princess of Draconia, I thank you for returning the gate key. With your help, I think we may mend relations between our peoples. From now on, I consider you a dragon friend."

"Oh!" Amy faltered, not sure what to say to that, but not wanting to offend the dragon. "That's nice. Um . . . when this is all over, maybe we can hang out together."

Opal's grin widened in amusement. "Something like that." She jabbed the shining key into a small hole where the gate doors latched together.

A surge of magic pulsed through the bars of the gate and crackled through the ground under their feet. The hairs on the back of Amy's neck stood on end and a shiver ran through her body.

Flax gasped and jumped, hovering in the air on blurring wings.

From the forest behind them, Amy could hear growls, rumbles, and stamping feet. Another clear trumpet blast rang through the trees.

Opal glanced back once, then withdrew the key.

The gate swung outward, as smooth and silent as fog drifting in the wind. All along its bars, hundreds of jewels sparkled in the light, flashing with every color of the rainbow. Before them lay the ancient cobblestone path to the Tree of Worlds.

# CHAPTER TWENTY-FIVE

"Hurry! They're coming!" the dragon growled, pushing Amy and Flax forward with one talon while she turned her scaly head back to watch the trail. The sound of approaching dragons was growing louder every moment.

Amy stumbled forward, still feeling weak in the knees from using her magic. As she passed through the jeweled gate, she looked back over her shoulder anxiously.

Over the crest of the slope, she glimpsed dragon smoke, flapping leathery wingtips, and bright-blue banners streaming from long slender poles. One of the banners caught the sunlight and a flash of metallic silver glinted from the fabric. With a start, Amy recognized the shining symbol emblazoned on the blue banner. It was the same tree that was etched into her talisman, the symbol of the royal family of Titania.

Before she could do or say anything, the gate swung to a close, sending out another surge of fierce magic that Amy felt through her whole body. She trembled at the sensation and turned back to Opal, shouting through the bars of the gate, "Don't hurt them, please! Those fairies are my friends. They came from the palace to save us!"

Opal lashed her tail with impatience and snorted. "I won't harm them unless they attack first. You have my word."

Amy exchanged a worried glance with Flax as a dozen dragons came into view on the other side of the gate. With them was a small group of fairies, including Zinnia, Bromeliad, and Hawthorne. In one hand, each carried a royal banner. In the other, their crystal-tipped spears sparkled with powerful magic.

Then Amy saw her mother. She strode up the hill behind the others with her face relaxed and neutral. Her hands were folded regally in front of her. The magic radiating out of her made her shine like a fallen star. It was hard to steadily gaze at her. Even from a distance, Amy could feel the power and determination Queen Lily radiated, more than enough to match the ferocity of any dragon.

"Oh, no!" Amy slapped her hand over her mouth in

horror. "My mom's here!"

Opal lashed her spiky tail and turned back to them with a hiss. "Hurry!"

When Amy still hesitated, Opal turned to glare at Flax. "Listen, fairy! You must understand. If you want to get to the tree, you must go now! Oaths may bind these others to act if they see your princess."

Amy was about to argue some more. Maybe she could talk to her mother. Maybe it would be all right if she could explain what was going on. If the queen knew that she and Flax only came to get the wood they needed, and that Princess Opal let them through the gate, surely everything would be all right.

Before she could get a word out, Flax grabbed her hand and pulled her after him, away from the gate and out of sight of the oncoming fairies and dragons.

"Flax?" she panted. "What are you doing? We should talk to them!"

"Not this time," Flax said, still dragging her along the path. "I agree with the dragon." He made a face like the words somehow tasted bad in his mouth.

"What? What do you mean? Why?"

They came around a bend in the path, and Flax slowed to a walk, releasing her hand. "I never thought I'd say those words in that order," he said, frowning, "but she's right. If we stayed to talk, things would get too complicated. They might even fight."

"But couldn't we just explain to them—"

He held up a hand. "Remember how you promised Orchid to get berries from the Tree of Worlds?"

She frowned. "Yeah . . ."

"Well, what would happen if you turned back now?"

Amy thought about it for a moment. Maybe it wouldn't be such a bad idea to go back. Queen Lily was right there, bursting with so much power that no dragon would dare challenge her. Amy could run back into her mother's arms and go back home. In a few hours, she'd be enjoying frothed honey milk and nut bread in her room in the palace. She and Flax could get some much-needed elixir. All their problems would be over.

As she considered the idea, a wave of foreboding rushed through her body, the sense that her doom was imminent. The sensation was so fierce, her gut wrenched with nausea. She choked, groaned, and staggered back to rest on the smooth white trunk of a fallen tree, wiping beads of sweat from her brow with her forearm.

The feeling was familiar. It was what the fairies called an onus. Her magical agreement with Orchid wouldn't let her back out now, even if she wanted to. She had to keep her word.

"Okay," she said, trying to shake off the sick feeling of mysterious danger. "I'll just tell my mother that I made a promise to Orchid. She wouldn't make us leave if she knew that."

"And what if all those fairies also swore an oath that they would bring us home at any cost?" Flax demanded. "That sounds like the kind of silly, dramatic thing my father would do. He wouldn't think that there might be a good reason to let us keep going, only that we need to be brought home no matter what."

Amy sighed and rubbed her hands along the smooth wood of the fallen tree. "That sounds like something my mother would do, too. And if they swore an oath like that, they wouldn't be able to let us go, even if we explained what we were doing."

"Also," Flax went on, "Princess Opal promised to hold them off for us. I don't know if magic binds dragons to their word like it does fairies, but they do seem to have some sense of honor. If the queen's guards tried taking us away, she might start fighting them for us. Then all those other dragons would probably join in."

Amy grimaced and buried her face in her hands. "What if they start fighting anyway? I wish I never made that promise and we never came here. I wish they stayed in Titania. How did they even find us?"

Flax sat next to her and wrapped an arm around her shoulders. "She's the fairy queen, Amy. It would take some pretty powerful magic to keep her from finding you. Did you really think she'd let us come here and not do anything about it?"

Amy buried her face in her hands again.

"But, hey! Since the queen is coming here to find a lost princess, the dragons might not fight her over it. They're bringing her here, so they haven't attacked her yet. I don't think the dragons want to go to war any more than the fairies do."

Amy stayed quiet for a moment, thinking over his words.

More than anything, she wanted to turn back and run to her mother, to keep the dragons from attacking her, to explain what they were trying to do and why.

"You returned the gate key, too," Flax went on. "That was the stolen treasure, the whole reason the last war happened. When Opal tells the dragon king you returned it, that should make things better between us. And she promised she wouldn't attack them unless they attacked her first."

Amy nodded, took a breath, and stood up. "Okay, let's get there as fast as we can. We're already past the gate, so the Tree of Worlds should be straight ahead. It shouldn't take too long to get there, right?"

Flax ran a hand through his hair and smiled. "Right. I'm sure we're still going to be in big trouble when we get back, though."

Amy chuckled weakly. "As long as we can make new fairy doors, it'll be worth it."

With a last sad look back toward the gate, they turned toward the looming Tree of Worlds and started walking. They followed the overgrown cobblestone path as it led through a grove of gnarled fruit trees, wove between thick, colorful bushes, and drew them gradually closer to the center of the walled garden.

"So . . . Amy, I've been wondering," Flax said, rubbing his hand on the back of his neck as they walked.

"What?"

"Do you realize what you did out there at the gate?"

"I healed the dragon, so she decided to be my friend?"

"Well, yeah. But that's not what I'm talking about."

"Oh." Amy winced. "You mean the part where I tried to kill her with the gate key."

"Amy . . . you used your magic. You made spells!"

Amy stopped and gasped in realization. She blinked and swallowed. "I did!"

"I knew you could do it!" Flax said, grabbing her shoulder and giving her a little shake. "I knew you just had to—"

"I finally figured out how to use my magic, and the first thing I did was try to kill the dragon princess!" Her eyes widened, and she clutched her throat in horror.

"What? No!"

"Does that make me some kind of monster?"

"Amy!"

Amy hugged herself and turned away. She remembered pouring her magic into a spell meant to rip through Princess Opal's flesh and destroy her. It had felt so natural. She hadn't even thought about it. Is that what it took for her to use her magic?

"Listen!" Flax said, shaking her shoulder again to get her attention. "That wasn't the first spell you did. Don't you remember? You used your magic to shield me from dragon's fire. That was a really impressive spell, and definitely not something a monster would do!" He rolled his eyes as though the thought that Amy could be a monster was ridiculous.

Amy relaxed her shoulders, remembering how her shield spell had blocked the dragon flames, saving Flax from certain annihilation.

"I knew you could do it! Especially after my spell to help you at the Mirror Pool worked so well."

"Yeah." She cocked her head at him curiously. "What was that spell you used on me?"

Flax shrugged his shoulders and chuckled. "Just a minor spell to lower your inhibitions . . . temporarily, of course. It made you feel confident, so you wouldn't worry about anything."

She raised an eyebrow at him. "Really?" She wasn't sure whether to feel grateful for the help or embarrassed. When that spell had been on her, she'd wanted to do some pretty silly things. "What do fairies use that spell for usually?"

Flax laughed. "We prank humans, of course. Especially the ones who try to capture us."

They laughed together and Amy let out a long, satisfied sigh. She could finally use her magic. She didn't have any to use at the moment, but that didn't matter. Just knowing that she wasn't somehow defective because she was half human was enough.

They continued walking along the path. The surrounding trees grew thicker, casting them in a dark shade that made it harder to see. Now and then, smooth bone-white wood, like the fallen tree she'd sat on earlier, flashed between the rustling dark leaves of the undergrowth. Curious, Amy stepped closer and parted the flowering bushes to see what it was.

"Wow. Flax! Come here. Look at this."

Flax peered over her shoulder to see. Together, their eyes followed the smooth white surface as it arched up, growing into a mound where it joined another. The thick cords of wood wound around the path, meeting others, growing thicker and taller still until they met with a wall of smooth, white, living wood like a frozen waterfall as big around as a football stadium.

"It wasn't a fallen tree at all," Amy said, staring. "What we were sitting on before . . ."

"It was just a root," Flax said, his voice hushed.

Together, they tipped their heads back to gaze up at the mountainous tree stretching overhead. Its topmost leaves were white with frost, like a mountaintop.

The size of it was not something she would have been able to describe in words to someone else. Even if she had a camera with her, a picture could not convey how big the tree was, or how small she felt standing under it. Looking at it made her feel dizzy. It reminded her of looking down into the Grand Canyon. She'd seen pictures before her father had taken her, but she never understood how big the canyon was until she was standing there, clutching the railing while her stomach did little flips in her gut and an eagle soared far below.

The sky overhead was dimming to a soft twilight, the colors around them shifting to gray and purple. Along the branches of the Tree of Worlds, the leaves glowed with a magical blue light that shone off the silvery-white trunk.

Tiny golden sparkles flashed between the leaves in the canopy, and Amy thought those must be the rowan berries. It was a rowan tree, just as Orchid had said it was, alive and growing in the realm of magic.

"It's so beautiful," Amy whispered, unable to look away.

"Of course it is," Flax whispered back. "It's the Tree of Worlds."

Fairies of Titania Book 3

# The Tree of Worlds

N.A. Davenport

# THE TREE OF WORLDS CHAPTER 1

The luminous Tree of Worlds towered overhead, and Amy gaped at it.

Since she'd lived in Titania for a few months, she was used to seeing trees as big as houses, broad enough to hold entire families within their trunks. But the Tree of Worlds was more like a mountain. Its gleaming branches stretched into the heavens, higher than any bird could fly. Each massive branch could fit an entire neighborhood of fairies. Silvery light shone from the delicate leaves, shimmering among the distant swaying limbs above.

Amy's eyes followed the smooth white trunk of the tree up, and up, and up until her head tilted back and her mouth fell open. Somewhere among those shimmering leaves high overhead, magical rowan berries grew, and Amy had to collect one to keep her promise. How was she going to do that? They were so far away!

Standing at her side, Flax fluttered his wings and let out a soft sigh. "So that's the Tree of Worlds. It really is a lot bigger than it looked from outside the garden, isn't it?" His voice was soft and weary.

Amy glanced over at her fairy friend. He looked tired from the strain of their adventure so far. His normally vibrant and colorful wings were flat and dull, resting folded against his back. He stood with a slight slouch, as though staying upright was tiresome.

"We should just get the rowan berry and a sliver of wood as fast as we can so we can go home. It looks like you need some elixir, and we're all out," she said.

Flax nodded and sighed again.

"You're a trained berry collector, right? Do you have any ideas how we can get a rowan berry from way up in the tree?"

Flax narrowed his eyes, searching the distant branches. "They are very high up. So high the air will probably be thin and cold. I'm sorry, I'm just too weak to fly up that far after everything." He glanced over at her and his mouth twitched into a crooked smile. "Also, I don't like the idea of leaving you alone down here. Who knows what kind of trouble you could get into?"

Amy planted her fists on her hips and scowled at him. "What do you mean? I'm the one who fought off a dragon just a little while ago. What could possibly happen?"

"Yes, you did fight off a dragon," Flax said, chuckling. "And it was very impressive. But you also got captured, stuck in an iron cage, and nearly cooked up for dinner. Remember that?"

Amy folded her arms and pursed her lips thoughtfully, then nodded, conceding the point as they resumed walking toward the enormous tree. "Okay, sure. But most dragons aren't allowed in this garden. And now that we're friends with Princess Opal, we shouldn't have any more trouble with them."

Flax snorted. "She called you her friend, not me. Don't think that just because you're friendly with the dragon princess that all dragons are going to get along with fairies now."

Amy grimaced and glanced down the path toward the entrance gate. The dragon princess and her mother, the queen of fairies, were out there locked in a confrontation. Her mother had come to Draconia with a bunch of armed fairies to retrieve Amy and Flax. Doing that was breaking a peace treaty that the dragons and fairies had agreed to for hundreds of years.

Would her new dragon friend really start fighting her mom? Would her mother really risk everything in a violent battle with powerful dragons just to get Amy back home?

She gulped. "In that case, we need to get what we came for fast so we can leave."

"And to do that, we need to stay together," Flax pointed out. "This place is full of powerful magic." He shuddered and hugged himself. "I can feel it all around us. In the air, in the ground. It's like I'm breathing it in."

Amy paused and quieted her mind, focusing on her sense of magic. Flax was right. The air tingled with pent-up magical energy, like a powerful static electrical charge ready to burst. Now that she was paying attention, she could feel her skin prickle and a constant shiver running along her nerves.

It wasn't like the magic she was used to in Titania. The magic there was fairy magic, familiar and comfortable, like a warm blanket on a cold rainy night.

The magic here felt more like an oncoming thunderstorm—looming, foreign, and intimidating. Not evil, really, but more like a force of nature, unfeeling and deadly.

She shuddered. "You're right. We need to get out of here. How about we get a piece of wood first, then we can worry about finding a rowan berry."

"Good idea," Flax agreed. "There are plenty of roots poking out of the ground. We might be able to shave off a piece of one of those."

While Amy needed a rowan berry to fulfill her onus to the former queen, Orchid—if she didn't fulfill her magical obligation, her own magic would turn against her and drive her mad—she thought getting a splinter of wood from the Tree of Worlds was far more important. The piece of wood was necessary to create new fairy doors to the human world. And new fairy doors were necessary for the fairies to make their magical elixir. Without elixir, the fairies would run out of magic, and fairies couldn't survive without magic.

The two friends hiked along the garden path, scanning the ground. Bone-white roots of the Tree of Worlds erupted from the earth all around, looking like hills of white marble pushing through the garden floor.

"There's one close to the path!" Amy said, pointing out one peeking out of the bushes ahead of them.

They approached the root and Flax pulled out his little stone dagger. They exchanged a quick nervous glance, then Flax stabbed his knife at the mound of wood.

The stone blade glanced off the unyielding root without even leaving a mark. Flax tried again, laying the sharp blade at an angle and pressing it in with a sawing motion. The knife slid along the surface of the wood without even scratching it.

"Do you want me to try?" Amy asked.

Flax arched an eyebrow at her, then shrugged, handing over his knife.

Amy attacked the root, stabbing and slicing at it with

the fairy blade, but nothing she tried made a dent in the smooth wood.

"I think it's the magic," Flax said. "It feels like the tree has a defensive spell to protect itself from damage."

Amy sighed and handed the knife back to him. "So what are we supposed to do? We can't just give up!"

"I don't know," Flax said. "You're the princess. What do you want to do?"

Amy straightened up, stretching her back as she looked along the path toward the mountainous tree, and sighed wearily.

She was exhausted. Maybe not as much as Flax was, but the journey through Dragon Island had been difficult. Only hours earlier, they'd escaped dragons who had been trying to cook her for an evening meal. They'd made a mad dash to get away from their festival with dragons chasing after them. Then, just when they thought they were safe, she'd had to fight a magical battle with Princess Opal. And she'd used a lot of her magic to heal the dragon princess after she'd won. All these things left her feeling like she needed a good meal and a long nap wrapped up in warm, fuzzy blankets.

But she had neither of those things right now. Only the path ahead, and the magical Tree of Worlds shining in the sky above.

"I guess we have to keep going," Amy said, her voice dull with weary resignation. "Maybe we'll have better luck when we get to the trunk. Or maybe we can find a broken stick dropped on the ground somewhere."

"Okay," Flax said, taking a deep breath as he tucked his knife back into his pouch. Then he rose to his feet, and they continued along the path together.

As they neared the trunk, the surrounding bushes grew larger and more colorful. Bright flowers blossomed among the leaves, glowing like candles in the shadows. Amy brushed her fingers against them, marveling at their beauty, and her fingertips came away dusted with luminous pollen that tingled with powerful magic. Thick succulents with fleshy leaves tinged in purple, blue, and red clustered along the ground. Tall plants that looked like bushy, bright-yellow feathers rustled with delicate fluff in the breeze. In an open area next to the base of the tree, the ground appeared to be covered in hundreds of tiny multicolored cotton balls. But when Amy reached out to touch one, the whole collection disappeared in a flash, sucked into tiny openings in their short stems.

"Let's try here, Amy," Flax called. He waved her over to a divot in the trunk of the tree.

Amy jogged over to him and looked. There were some tiny scratch marks in the wood there already, as though some animal had used the divot as a foothold for its claws while climbing.

"Yeah, let's try it."

Flax drew his stone knife again and pressed the blade against the wood, pushing with all his might. But the blade didn't even leave a mark. He let out a frustrated breath of air and shook his head. "It's no good. I can't do it. Do you want to try again?"

Amy frowned and pressed her hand against the tree, trying to get a sense of the strange magic that protected it. Being only half fairy, she wasn't sure whether she could sense everything going on. But what she did feel was very powerful, like a tightly woven steel cage surrounding the tree—a steel cage with a series of heavy locks to keep anyone from opening it.

"The spell protecting the tree is really strong, and really complicated," she said.

"Do you think you can understand the magic? Well enough to change it?"

Amy's brow furrowed, and she answered carefully. "I think I could, eventually. I know I figured out how to use my magic. But, Flax, I still don't know how to do complicated spells like this."

"Maybe you could learn. I could teach you some spells! Maybe practicing would help you work on the spell of the tree."

Amy shook her head and pulled her hand away. "I think that would take a super long time. The spell is just too complicated. If I understood magic better, I might be able to make the tree soft enough to cut. But that's like saying if I understood cars better, I could build one. Whatever magic this tree has, it's way too hard for me right now." She sighed and leaned against the trunk. "Also, my magic is really low. I used so much of it fighting off dragon fire and healing Princess Opal, and now I'm down to my last drops."

Flax's face scrunched up in displeasure at the mention of Princess Opal. With the way fairies viewed dragons as evil, destructive monsters, Amy wasn't surprised. And it wasn't like the fairy perspective was unreasonable. Every dragon that they'd met on Dragon Island had attempted to eat or kill them. Even Princess Opal had at first.

They sat in silence together for several minutes, leaning against the base of the mountain-sized Tree of Worlds, with the sun sinking lower toward the horizon and the light shifting to soft gold.

"Well, we might as well look around for a stick or a fallen rowan berry before it gets dark," Amy suggested. She sort of hoped Flax would talk her out of it. What she really wanted to do was eat a big meal and go to sleep.

But her friend only nodded in agreement and pushed away from the tree. "You're right. There's no point sitting around. We should keep trying."

So they started picking their way over the ground, following the smooth wall of the trunk of the tree, hoping to find what they came for.

CONTINUE the adventure with Amy and Flax in THE TREE OF WORLDS, the third book in the Fairies of Titania series.

THANK you for reading THE DRAGON KEY. If you enjoyed this story, please leave a review. Reviews help other readers find books they like, and they fill authors' lives with joy.

Also by N. A. Davenport

## WEREWOLF MAX

Lost in the Graveyard

Werewolf Max and the Midnight Zombies

Werewolf Max and the Banshee Girl

Werewolf Max and the Monster War

## FAIRIES OF TITANIA

The Last Fairy Door

The Dragon Key

The Tree of Worlds

## DRAGON RIDERS OF AVRIA

Anri and the Dragon Quest

Secret of the Dragon Egg

Dragon Wings

Made in the USA
Las Vegas, NV
26 November 2024